{ DELPHINE PUBLICATIONS PRESENTS }

"Tamika Newhouse pens the best fiction
with characters so real you'll swear you know them."
- *New York Times bestselling author Mary B Morrison*

THE Words I DIDN'T Say

"Always choose love in everything that you do"

TAMIKA NEWHOUSE

AUTHOR OF IF I AIN'T THE ONE YOU LOVE

The Words I Didn't Say

Delphine Publications focuses on bringing a reality check to the genre Published by Delphine Publications

Delphine Publications focuses on bringing a reality check to the genre urban literature. All stories are a work of fiction from the authors and are not meant to depict, portray, or represent any particular person Names, characters, places, and incidents are either the product of the author's imagination or are used fictitiously, and any resemblances to an actual person living or dead are entirely coincidental

ISBN: 978-0996084499

Edited by: Tee Marshall
Layout: Write On Promotions
Cover Design: TSP Creative

Printed in the United States of America

To the man who taught me so much about love passed those high school love letters.
For Driskell

"The biggest coward of a man is to awaken the love of a woman without the intention of loving her."

\- Bob Marley

Before their souls said goodbye....

I've been so many places in my life and time. I've sung a lot of songs and made some bad rhymes. I've acted out my life in stages with ten thousand people watching. But we're alone now and I'm singing this song to you - Donny Hathaway

I studied her face as Donny's voice crooned through the night's air. This song fit perfectly with how I was feeling right now. She was the perfect woman, the perfect wrong for me. I was wrong myself and I knew that. Selfish in so many ways that I expected her to accept my faults in spite of her pain. She loved me and I loved her, and tonight I wanted to express just how much.

She was so beautiful, young, vibrant, and wounded just as I. I smiled slightly and focused in on her eyes. She sat there only mere inches away from my lips and breathed in deep. I laughed a little because she could be dramatic at times. She loved hard and I loved that about her. But I loved hard too and that scared me to death because I had only loved once and that didn't work out.

"Don't compare me to her. Don't compare me with your past. I can't win that battle because it's already done. But I can win your future." Janet would beg of me often to just be in the moment.

I leaned toward her, our noses pressed against each other. I matched her breathing and hummed. "I love you."

Her eyes became glossy, her body grew tense, and she was beginning to fight that feeling again. Love. We both fought love. She once told me, "I don't wish to fight my feelings for you I just can't help it."

I had planned this night out perfectly. In one of the most beautiful hotels in downtown Atlanta, the best food, the prettiest rose petals covered the floors, the brightest candles lit our room and I set the mood with Donny Hathaway. I had done things like this before to woo a woman, but Janet was different.

"I love you babe," I told her again.

Her tears were evident as she challenged herself to look at me head on. Her face was solemn. She seemed at peace. "I waited twenty-nine years for someone like you. For someone to get me, and here you are. It's surreal you know. For me to love you," she whispered. I studied her words as I always did.

"Yes babe I know."

"Things like this don't last forever. Things like this only happen in the movies," she added.

"Stop fighting me." I sat down my glass of wine and placed my hand on her shoulders. Forcing her body to face mine and to stare me head on. I gave her a slight shake. "Babe stop fighting me."

"Why not fight Denim? Why just allow these feelings to build? We are allowing them to build into what?"

I dropped my hands into my lap, leaned backwards, and examined her question. "I am not a fortune teller. I don't know what to tell you."

"We had an agreement. You remember that right?"

I shook my head yes. I knew what she meant and I didn't think she completely trusted me anyhow. I didn't blame her because I knew what type of man I was. Here I was over the age of thirty-five with the perfect woman that seemed to be made from my very rib and I didn't want just her. I still desired other women. I wanted the chance to continue to be a whore. The whore I have been since I could remember.

She was perfect for me in all the wrong ways and the very fact that she was made for me scared me. Because she was everything that I ever wanted in a woman and I knew that I could very well break her heart made her wrong for me. Her perfection challenged my selfishness. So we made an agreement. But agreements are made to be broken, right?

Janet sat her drink down and leaned backwards on the bed's headboard. "This was nice what you did." Her eyes traveled across the room examining the ambiance of the love I attempted to create.

"Thank you babe."

"This night, well this day was perfect. I do love you Denim. You know that right?"

"Yes babe I know."

"Let's just keep it simple ok."

She grabbed her wine and took a huge swallow. I don't know why her words pierced me but they did. It was as if I wanted her to tell me she only wanted me. I wanted her to say that she was ready to go to the next level so that we could build a life together. But she didn't. Instead she said the same words I always professed. But often times I was torn.

I could manage the thought of her being with another man as long as I had free reign to be with other women and that is what we have been doing for months now. It would be a year soon and we were still stuck in this limbo of 'I love you but not enough to only want you'.

Straight bullshit if you ask me, but we were both stuck in our selfish desires. It was easy before I met her. Life was simple. I didn't want another relationship. I didn't want another friend. I really didn't want another woman. It was the mere fact that I still held onto my own freedom, my sense of 'I can do what the fuck I want' that kept us in this space.

If I opened my mouth right now and said, "Babe I only want you," would she even believe me? I was Denim Overton. A whore by blood, a man without bounds, a selfish man, no kids, no wife, no soul. I was a man who had loved once and fucked it over because I chose the desires of my dick more. And now I sat across from the person I loved who shared my very same past . She too had a broken heart just as I did.

We couldn't trust each other. Or could we? "Babe I agree let's just enjoy tonight, us, let's just do that." I stood up and marched into the bathroom and splashed water across my face. I saw her shrug her shoulders as I walked away as if she was convincing herself she didn't care. I know she did though because I did too. If I said I didn't care maybe I could feel that same way too. But pride wouldn't let me say it.

I walked back into the room and smiled at Janet. This way was fine; at least she was in my life. "Let's eat babe."

She looked up towards me and smiled. "Good because all this mushy shit has caused me to want to eat a whole cow." She scooted off the bed and I followed her into the dining area where we ate and talked all night. We enjoyed each other's company and we were the best of friends. Such good friends that we knew what wasn't being said.

We had agreed no strings. But the day we said hello our strings became attached. She had become my lifeline and I hers.

THE *Words* I Didn't Say

Janet

I looked over at my client blankly and blew out hot air. "But sir I've already explained the process. These things don't happen overnight. You have to allow me to do my job. This is what I do." Regardless of what I was saying, he wasn't hearing me. I stood up from my seat and said, "Let's just meet in three days. We can decide to go from there if you choose to."

I watched him walk out just as soon as Claire walked in. "Girl what happened with him?"

I rolled my eyes and waved her off. "He needs to understand I am a natural born writer. I can write this damn memoir but it's going to be done my way. His trying to dictate this process is annoying as hell. Anyway are we still going to the Mocha Café tonight? Let me know because I will have to leave here early."

"Yeah I have to go, one of my clients is performing and it would be good research for me and I can add it in the book."

I blew out hot air and dropped my head into my hand. "That reminds me I have to go and see this singer guy and meet with his manager. I don't feel like doing this mess tonight."

Claire sat down on the edge of my desk and laughed. "Okay Ms. Professional. You got this. This is our busiest season and we got to finish up these projects to get the next deal. Money and duty calls boo boo."

"I still haven't finished my own damn novel." I sat standing up from my desk and throwing papers into my briefcase.

"But the point is you will, find the time and stop entertaining all these random men you're dealing with,"

I stopped midstride, stared at her and laughed. "Why not? It's fun you should try it."

"No thanks I'll just stick to my one."

I looked around my office and checked to ensure I had everything that I needed.

"Okay, I will see you at the café after this meeting."

"Are you headed there now?" Claire asked running behind me as I walked out into our office building's hallway.

"Yes ma'am. I'm actually behind."

"Cool grab me a banana nut cupcake from Lily's Bakery on your way to the café please."

I laughed at Claire. "Fine greedy ass. I'm out. I'll see you tonight." I leaned in and gave her a kiss and hopped on the elevator.

€€€

I walked into the restaurant and asked the hosts for the party of a Denim Overton. She assured me that my party called and said they would be five minutes late and led me to my table. I knew that at meetings like this my bill was always covered by the client so I wasted no time ordering an appetizer and pulling out my laptop to work on my novel.

Thirty minutes and fifteen hundred words, and a plate full of bones later, I heard, "Janet Jamison?"

My eyes traveled over my laptop and trailed from the soles of the most expensive shoes I would never spend money on, up his leg, briefly stopping at his mid-section to examine the bulge but I made sure to not stare too long. His torso was broad; his arms were dark so he was a chocolate brother. Please let him be cute please let him be cute. I stared at his face and tilted my head to the side. Got damn this man is sexy.

Stuttering over my words and attempting to gain my composure I say, "Yes!"

2

He extended his hand and said, "Denim Overton. I do apologize for my tardiness. You can never be too sure with Atlanta's traffic."

I suddenly heard the sounds of "Freak Me" by Silk but I think it was only in my head. "Oh that's fine. I had some time to write."

He took a seat across from me and smiled. "You're the writer that everyone praises up in New York. They say you're the best."

I blushed. "They speak truth. I've already been looking into your client's life. I think this project is going to be a quick and easy one. He is pretty much an open book."

"Yeah he is someone I can't control and he is pretty open." He said, referring to his client.

"I thought he was going to join us too?"

After ordering a drink Denim turned his attention back to me and said, "No, he had a show in Tampa so he left this morning. I didn't want to cancel because we have pushed this back long enough. Tell me what you have in mind."

I begin to lay out the idea for the memoir I was going to write for his artist. I had written for indie and mainstream artists and actors a dozen times and I was good at what I did. So good that my best friend, Claire, and I decided to open our own offices called From the Pen of Claire and Janet . We were both published authors, but we were currently working as ghostwriters for a lot of celebrities throughout the Atlanta area. For this project with Denim's artist I would pocket over $75,000. So was I complaining truly about being behind on my own project? No. But then again I wrote for the love of it not just for the dollar sign.

"You are good," Denim said, just above a slight laugh. He leaned back in his seat as our server sat a plate of salmon and rice in front of him.

"I try to do my best," I said, as my plate of turkey and dressing was placed before me. "Have you read any of my works? Tell me what you know about me."

3

THE **I Didn't Say**

He raised an eyebrow. "Well I actually have been in Houston a lot working on an album with an artist so I haven't been out of the cave in about two months. I hadn't had the chance to do much of anything else."

"Oh so what do you do when you're in the studio?"

"I create beats. The sound of the music."

"Oh that's right?" I smiled and nodded my head while covering my mouth that was full of food. "You're DJ Denim O!"

He had a look of shock on his face. I didn't know why so I asked, "Thought I wouldn't know about you?"

"Depends on what you heard."

He took a bite of his food keeping his eyes glued to mine. I had to rearrange myself in my seat. Denim was more than handsome. He was so heavy on my eyesight that I took deeper breaths to maintain the anxiety building in between my legs.

"Well, I heard some things from back in the day. You've been in the game for a while now, huh?"

"Ten years," he said, leaning back in his seat. "Started in small clubs back in Fort Worth, Texas."

"Pause!"

He raised an eyebrow. "What?"

"I'm from there you know."

He gave me the side eye and smiled. I nearly sunk in my seat. I could feel juices from the crevices of my lips seep through and threaten to wet my panties. I squeezed my pelvis really tight hoping my efforts to tighten my walls would create a stopper to the flow. "Why are you looking at me like that?"

"You're from Funkytown?"

"Yes. I've been here in Atlanta for about five years now. Came here for my career."

"Small freaking world," he laughed.

"Small freaking world," I added.

There was an obvious pause in our exchange. I was too busy focusing on stopping the flow of my juices, but what the hell he was doing, I didn't know. I was thinking to myself this man was

4

obviously irresistible and he knew it. He sat there looking as if he possessed the most sought after tool in the world. Hmmmm his tool. I wonder.

I shook the thoughts out of my head and asked, "So you stay here?"

"I am in and out of almost every major city at some point. Nowhere is home really but Texas."

He stared at me. His stare was like dare. I couldn't tell what he was thinking. He had these seemingly innocent eyes that held a hint of grey.

"I like it here. It's different from Texas," I said.

"Very different. It's a city of opportunities you know… And meetings such as this."

I smiled and bowed my head as if I was a shy school aged girl when his cell phone buzzed. He glanced at the caller ID with a look of anxiousness. After apologizing for having to take the call, he picked up as I attempted to tune out his conversation. Although being nosey and writing about other people's lives was how I made a living, for once I wasn't trying to be.

Denim hung up and said, "I have to get to my next meeting but Janet I will definitely be in touch. I will let my client know what we came up with. He's really excited about this opportunity."

I stood up and shook Denim's hand. When my hand landed in his I felt a rush of something. It was weird. I couldn't explain why my palms became moist, my breathing became heavy, my heart began to race, and my mind was boggled. Denim tilted his head to the right and frowned. He feels it too.

I quickly let go of his hand and allowed it to drop to my side. "It was nice meeting you Denim."

His confused look didn't change as he stated, "It was a pleasure Ms. Jamison." He slowly took a few steps backwards until he turned on his heels and walked out of the restaurant. I plopped down into my seat and blew out hot air. What the hell just happened? I think I stared at my computer screen for ten minutes before I managed to collect my items and head out of the

THE [illustration] I Didn't Say

restaurant pushing back what was obvious; I wanted that man in the worst way.

Denim

"Forever and always," I said before hanging up the phone with my best friend. I made a stop in Sandy Springs before I had to make my way to the airport. I was prepping to expand my business by building a studio here. I had worked with some of the music industry's most successful rappers and singers and was now leaning towards the business end. That's where you make the most money anyway, in creating lanes for other people to make you money.

I walked in to see my business partner Dalvin directing the crew on what needed to be done. "Yo Dalvin update me," I said, without as much as a hello.

"These slow ass workers got us two weeks behind. I got it under control though D, don't trip."

I placed my fist into my right hand and gave it a squeeze. "Two weeks, that's going to cost me too much money. Make it happen. I don't want this shit delayed any further. I have a few clients who have their artists scheduled to make music here. Time is money dog." I eyed him and he reassured me that I didn't have to worry about anything.

"I have to hit the skies to Miami though," I added.

"When? Is Lena going with you?"

I eyed him and laughed. "No fucking way dog! Lena would be blocking all the ass I could get and I need a fucking release this week. I am stressed the hell out." •

Dalvin walked into his completely renovated office and went to his refrigerator. "Don't fuck that one up dog, Lena is actually a good one."

"I know; you keep telling me this shit because you messed things over with your wife. But hell, I told you once you partnered up with me; that marriage shit was over with anyway. No man can stay married in my crew."

Dalvin didn't respond, as usual. He had been my best friend since grade school. We grew up together in Fort Worth, Texas he knew all my secrets. He knew all of the women I left behind, he knew of the one woman I loved but let get away. He had gotten married almost ten years ago and but it failed about three years ago. He had become me. A womanizer. Hell, it wasn't my fault; he knew the rules of the road and took that shit home. He fucked up, not me.

"How long will you be in Miami?" He asked, changing the subject.

"A couple days. Got a few meetings and then I'll be back."

We gave each other a one-hand shake and said our goodbyes as I grabbed my luggage out of my office and headed out. My life was consistently on the run; I hated it and loved it at the same time. I dropped my briefcase rushing towards the elevators. Cursing under my breath, I reached down to collect my items and stuffed them back inside when I came across her book.

Janet Jamison.

The business associates who referred me to her had given me one of her novels. I flipped it over and for the first time I noticed her picture on the back cover. I felt myself sink as if I was standing on quicksand. She was beautiful. It was as if she was the most beautiful woman in the world . Something about her made her rare to me. Her smile, her darkened plum lips, her chocolate complexion, her long jet black hair. I paused and closed my eyes. It was then I could hear her laugh.

I jerked my eyes open. What the hell are you doing dog? I looked around the room I stood in to see if anyone noticed me on the ground daydreaming as if I just had the greatest nut in my life. I noticed that I was smiling and I frowned at that. I didn't want to smile. What the hell was I smiling about? She was just another chick. Man up and handle your business man.

I threw her book back into my bag and hopped up as the elevator opened. I shook her out of my head and made a mental note to make sure I utilized every source in Miami to not think about her. The first woman I saw that I wanted would get the end of all my current frustration. And my plan worked or at least I thought it did.

Janet

"I do not want to wear this tight ass dress Claire. Get this hot mess off of my bed. How dare you encourage me to wear this?" I laughed as I threw the dress at her. "I'm going to wear this one." I pulled out a simple black dress and red pumps.

Claire yawned, "I swear you are predictable. I can always predict what it is you're going to wear half of the time."

"So!" I said, slipping into my undergarments. I next sprayed on my Prada perfume and smirked at Claire as I continued dressing.

"Well, I guess it's been working for you so who am I to complain." She rose up and walked into my closet.

"Finally. Yes leave me be." I ran to my cell once I heard the ringing and clicked talk. "Hello."

"Hey baby." It was Paul. I purred at the sound of his voice. The man had the mouth of God. I called him my headhunter because no one ate me out like him.

"Paul baby what's up, how are you?"

"I'll be better if I get to see my kitty tonight."

I laughed and purred loudly. "Tonight?"

"Yes baby tonight. I need you." He practically sounded like a school age boy begging for his first kiss. Claire walked out of my closet with shoes in tow and rolled her eyes. I placed my index finger on my lips to signal for her to not make a sound.

"I think I can do that, but I have to go to this gathering love. How about I call you as soon as I get home? Is that okay, can you wait for me?" I asked in a seductive tone.

"Okay baby I'll be waiting."

I blew a kiss to the phone and pressed the end button. When I saw my line was clear I leaned upward and walked over to my dress to put it on.

"You crack me the hell up." Claire fell back onto my bed in laughter. I turned and looked over towards her.

"What the hell is so funny?" I smirked.

"Poor Paul. You got that man in love and shit and you over here getting ready for a date. Who is your date with tonight?"

"Kelvin," I said and licked my lips. Kelvin was a successful lawyer who had an office in Midtown. He stood 6'2" and made it look sexy as hell, perfectly built, and was caramel tasty.

"Oh!" Claire rolled her eyes and placed my shoes on her feet.

"I know you don't like him but he's fun. He gets my busy schedule and when we're together its magic."

"Yeah, but when you're not he's a whore. I can't stand his ass."

"And what am I Claire? I have a rolodex of men just waiting for me. Am I a whore too?" Claire paused and then turned her attention away from me.

"No, you're just hurt. Big difference. "

I threw up my hand and yelled out, "Stop! Not tonight. Do not mention that man tonight. Okay?"

Claire jumped off my bed and smiled. "You look beautiful sis, let's go so we won't be late."

€€€

The room at the Lux Lounge was decorated beautifully. The aura was laced with colors of red and golden brown. The chandelier sparkled brightly creating an angelic ambiance in the room. It was another industry party full of Atlanta's elite socialites. I cuffed Kelvin's arm as we made our way around the room networking and talking to people we knew. I was always in the networking mood because everyone felt they had a book they wanted written and they knew that Claire and I were at the top of the list to write it.

"You want a glass of wine?" Kelvin asked eyeing the bar.

"Sure. You know my classic red please." He smiled, kissed me on my cheek, and walked away in the direction of the bar.

I found a place to stand off away from moving traffic but where Kelvin could find me when I heard, "You look amazing tonight."

The hairs on the back of my neck stood up as my heart began to beat an irregular rhythm. I knew that voice but I had to have been mistaken. No way was it him. I kept my position of where I stood but turned my head to look over my shoulder. "Denim!"

Had it only been a matter of days since I had seen him? Yes, it had been but I felt as if I was just with him.

"You look amazing Janet." He leaned in to embrace me and immediately I felt my knees weaken.

What in the world was it that caused my body to react this way to him? Not just my body, but my mind, the very rhythm of my heartbeat was different when I was in his presence. "You look amazing yourself." I managed to say as we released one another.

And I wasn't embellishing on that either. Denim looked extra dapper tonight. He was a gorgeous man. Denim stood over six feet, dark chocolate skin, muscular thick frame; he wore his hair low fade with the cutest waves. His full beard reflects Idirs Elba's swag. And his smile, Lord this man had a beautiful set of white teeth. He had a few buttons open of his silk shirt that was a plum purple and just the mere sight of his flesh there had me wet, black slacks, and black leather shoes. His black diamond watch was an obvious match to his level of class. He was rich. His demeanor spoke money.

"What are you doing here?"

He leaned on the wall next to me and exhaled, "Networking I guess. My publicist put me on the list so I had to come and show my face. This isn't my thing really."

"Your publicist has a good angle going I guess. You are new to the area sort of. You need to build connections." He nodded his head as if it was routine to hear this and laughed. "Heard this before huh?"

He eyed me and gave me the look that said obviously yes. "What are you drinking? You want me to get you something?"

"My friend is," I said, pointing towards Kelvin's direction and noticed him walking towards us. "Oh he's coming." Denim stood up quickly as if we were doing something we weren't supposed to be doing and looked over towards Kelvin.

"Oh! Hmmm," he mumbled something and I eyed him.

"What?" I placed my hands on my hips and playfully charged my body towards his. He rose up his hands in laughter.

"Calm down little lady. Just noticing your little fella walking over that's all. But yeah we will talk soon." He placed his right hand on the small of my back and kissed my cheek. "Have a good night Janet."

I pressed my cheek against his lips and smirked. "I sure will," I mouthed back. He smiled and walked away in the direction he came from as my eyes followed him. I was so stuck on not wanting him to leave my sight that I jumped at the sound of Kelvin's voice.

"Who was that?" Kelvin asked handing me my glass of wine.

"A client. Working on a new memoir, that's all."

He took a sip from his glass and raised an eyebrow curiously. "Seemed like you two were old friends or something."

I eyed him. "Denim and I? No way," I said, pointing towards my chest. I noticed the uncomfortable high pitch in my voice and made a mental note to get it together. "He's just from my hometown so we talked about that before. Other than that, he's just a 10client."

THE I Didn't Say

Kelvin didn't press the issue. We made our way to a dinner table where I spotted Claire and her husband Evan. I leaned in and hugged them both. Taking a seat next to Claire she whispered in my ear, "The smile you had with that mystery man was like no other and Kelvin saw it. Who was that? Spill it."

I eyed her and took a deep breath. My eyes were filled with excitement and fear at the same time. Because I knew I liked Denim but what I was feeling was more than I just want to bang your brains out. "Him; that's the guy I can't get out of my head."

Denim

"She's beautiful right?" I eyed Dalvin who was nose deep in his plate.

"Yo dog, what the hell? You haven't even touched your plate talking about that damn woman. She's with someone. Let it go."

I turned around in my seat and took my attention back to my plate. "Yeah you're right. So what are we getting into after this? I swear this here is boring." I whispered not wanting the other table guest to hear me.

"There's a listening party at the Lime Studios tonight. A few artists will be there. That's what Lena has scheduled for you." He said, mentioning my personal assistant and my on and off again girlfriend.

Dalvin looked up from his plate and joked, "Your girl is on the move."

I don't know why I frantically turned around in my seat as if my body was under attack but I did. The very thought of Janet moved me. Where is she going? My eyes followed her as she walked towards the back of the room and when I couldn't see her any longer I stood up. Without turning around to face Dalvin I said, "Be right back."

I marched across the room trying not to look obvious and I glanced over towards the table Janet where had been sitting to see if her guy was watching me. He wasn't but the woman seated next to Janet was. She gave me a slight smile. I gave her a slight smile back.

As I made my way to the back, I noticed it was the bathroom area. I looked for the sign marking the ladies room.

THE [] I Didn't Say

There! I quickly snuck up to the door and noticed it was a one person stall. Perfect!

Leaning against the wall, I waited for her to open the door. When I heard the water turn on and off I felt my heart jump into my throat. The intense anxiety that was boiling through my veins was becoming overwhelming. I don't know what I was planning to do. I don't even know why I walked back here. I just knew that she was here and that's where I needed to be.

When I heard the door unlock and the knob turn I leaned up and stood in the doorway. She jumped in fear and brought her hand to her chest. "Denim!" She whispered. I grew weak. I felt it travel down my spine to my lower back and now to my knees. The sound of my name out of her mouth weakened me. I rushed into the bathroom placing my right hand on her belly pushing her back into the room.

I turned and locked the door. She eyed me. Her brown eyes were wide, bold, and confused. She eyed me, then the door, and then repeated. I stood there in front of her in that small room my breathing rapid as if I had just run a mile. The palms of my hands were sweaty as I rubbed them on my pants.

"Janet!" I whispered. Upon saying her name her shoulders began to sink. Her eyes became misty; her mouth slightly fell open and quivered.

"Yes," she whispered back. I took two steps closer to her. I moved toward her slowly like a lion moving in on its prey. Our breathing was now matched. I moved at a slower steady pace but my flesh was boiling hot.

I leaned my head downward to look directly into her eyes. She was reading me. Her eyes were moving rapidly across my face as if she were taking mental pictures of me.

"I...I..." I didn't know what to say. What do you say in a moment like this? I felt something for this woman. What was it?

Janet dropped her head back so that she could look directly up to me and then she smiled. Not so obvious but her eyes

10

lit up with brightness. Her cheeks slightly curved to the shape of her face and her lips smiled at me.

"Hi," she whispered.

"Hi," I whispered back. Trailing my hands up her arms, I pulled her closer to me. Our bodies now pressed together I just stared at her. I studied the desire in her eyes. And then I did something I'd wanted to do since the first moment I heard her laugh. I leaned down and covered my lips with hers.

Our moans were evident as our kisses became the kiss. The one kiss that breathed life into my body. Her lips felt as if they were designed to fit in between mine. With pecks, licks, and full mouth embraces I made love to her mouth. My moans were the assurance she would need to know that this was the kiss of my life. She was the kiss of my life. I think I needed her before I even knew that I did.

A knock on the door jerked us out of our trance. "Oh my God." Janet began to look around hysterically. "We can't stay in here." She covered her mouth as if she wanted to hide the fact that we had just kissed.

"Come with me." I shocked myself with that statement as she just stared at me.

"I…I can't do that tonight. Let's just talk later okay?" Janet rushed around me as I turned around and followed her.

"Wait." I grabbed her wrist as she placed her hand on the doorknob.

"Denim we have to get out of this bathroom."

I read her eyes. It was as if she were begging me to let her go. The mist that now covered her brown colored eyes was weird. It wasn't happiness. It wasn't desire. I recognized that look because I have felt it many times before. It was fear. It was sadness. I released her wrist as I felt I had just looked myself in the eyes.

She hurriedly opened the door and walked out. I followed behind her as a lady wanting to use the bathroom walked in. "Oh sorry ma'am. It's all yours." She looked at me in shock and with a judgmental stare. I ignored her and walked out into the lounge. I looked over towards Janet who was preparing to leave.

THE ~~Shit~~ I Didn't Say

I made my way back to Dalvin and felt anger succumb me. "Ready to go?"

Dalvin searched my face and asked, "You aight man, you don't look good."

"The listening party right, let's get there." I said ignoring his question. He did what I asked and we were off to the next event.

Janet

"You haven't said anything on the ride home Janet, are you okay?" I heard Kelvin ask me as I stared out of the window.

"Just tired. I have a long day tomorrow." He pulled up in front of my house and my hand was on the car door to open it even before he came to a complete stop. "I'll call you tomorrow ok." I didn't wait for him to respond before I hopped out. He called after me but I just waved him off.

I stayed in a nice home in Marietta about twenty minutes from downtown Atlanta. Four bedrooms, fully renovated basement, three baths. It was a large house for one woman. A month would go by and there would be rooms I would never even walk in, but I loved the space and I loved the neighborhood. It was home for me.

I cut on the living room light and threw my keys on the table designated for my mail. I kicked off my shoes and set the house alarm. I marched into the kitchen, pulled my vanilla bean Blue Bell ice cream out of the freezer, and found the biggest spoon in my utensil drawer.

I took a huge bite and dropped it in my mouth. Walking into my bedroom, I plopped down on my bed and ignored Kelvin's calls. I knew he just wanted to see what was wrong. I texted a response instead of picking up. I knew there would be consequences to my behavior tonight but at this moment I didn't care. I was lost in my thoughts.

After twenty minutes went by I finally picked up my cell phone and scrolled through my texts. I noticed Paul reaching out to me. I smiled and text him back. I needed him to come over and offer up a distraction.

THE ~~HEAD~~ I Didn't Say

"I'll be there in twenty minutes baby," he told me.

I hopped up and took a quick shower. I knew that tonight I would get the release I so needed.

When I heard two knocks on my front door I jumped up in excitement. My clit engorged on cue because I was anticipating his touch there. I was ready for that explosive release. I opened the door and smiled. "Paul!"

Paul walked in. His average height almost matched mine but he was cute. He did things to me that I loved to feel physically. He even embraced the nickname I gave him, Head Hunter. He was only a year older than me, yellow as the sun is bright with the darkest black hair, and he was a smooth talker too. He would smooth talk me right out of my panties.

He hugged me tightly and buried his face in my neck, "Hey baby."

"Go ahead and go into the room while I go grab us some glasses and some wine." He kissed me on my lips and followed my orders.

I had retrieved my items and was back in my room within thirty seconds. "Baby I missed you!" I stopped in my tracks as my mouth dropped in anticipation.

"Well hello to you too."

Paul stood beside my bed one leg hiked up on the post while his dick hung very low between his widened legs. There he stood naked as the day he was born. I moaned and bit my bottom lip giving him the head to toe assessment. "Babe you are too fine."

I placed the glasses and wine down on my dresser as he signaled for me to come closer. "Come here." He grabbed my hand and aggressively pulled me into him. He roughly kissed my lips and then commanded me to lie face down.

He turned me over and pushed me down on my bed, my face buried in my comforter I could feel his hands becoming familiar with my curves. He moaned, "How has my baby been?"

"I've been so bad Daddy. So very bad," I purred. Paul pulled up my negligee and gave my tight ass slap. He moaned and I could hear the smacking of his lips.

I arched my back and I felt Paul lower himself on top of me kissing my flesh through my negligee. I widened my legs to release some of the pressure that had built up there. My clit was fat, so fat it was now pushing its way through my lips as my thick cream oozed through. I cried out for Paul to taste me. I needed that release. I was damn near in convulsions. I could feel his dick slide down my back in between my ass cheeks and now my thighs.

His face was now buried in my ass crack. He grunted loudly and sniffed deep as if he was searching for a hidden treasure. I screamed at the sting from him ripping my panties from my flesh. He angrily pushed my face back down in the bedding. I loved this shit; I thought as he spread my ass and gave my hole a deep suck.

Paul hated for me to move when he was handling his business and I loved to move just so he could punish me. But I squeezed my pelvis real tight this time to not disobey him. I didn't want his tongue to move from its position. My face was buried in the bedding when Paul lifted my legs over his shoulder. Ass in the air and my kitty staring him directly in his face. He slowly leaned forward and kissed my lips.

I knew my cream was oozing and dripping from his lips now. I began to shake as he gave me more sweet kisses there. I felt like my clit would burst into pieces. It was so swollen it had become unbearable.

Paul opened my lips, wrapped his mouth around my pearl tongue, and gave it a rough tug. I squirmed and cried out. He sucked and licked and sucked and licked, dipping his tongue in and out of me. I felt my juices squirt all over Paul's face in one massive explosion. He didn't give me time to catch my breath as he continued to taste me. I squeezed my bedding tightly then hooked my legs around his neck and embraced the ride. I loved my Head Hunter.

Claire

I walked into my home office and studied the computer screen for what seemed like a century. I wasn't in the mood for writing. I wasn't in the mood for being in this house. I was ready to just go out and run my worries away. That's what I would do, run.

I hopped up from my desk and ran upstairs to put on my running gear. It was a perfect spring day and the running trail traced around his beautiful lake. I had run it since we moved into this house a year ago. I lived in a quiet multimillion home division in Roswell. Evan, my husband, owned a few Audi dealerships throughout the area. To say he was often busy was an understatement. A part of me wanted to hurry up and finish my novel so that I could go back on tour. I hated being home alone but Evan didn't seem to mind it.

I picked up my phone and text Janet. She responded that she would be in the office around two. I made a mental note to be there around the same time. I put on my stopwatch and ran out of the house.

When the breeze hit my flesh I felt peace. I smiled brightly and picked up my speed heading towards the lake. My headphones were on full blast as I listened to the sounds of Hil St. Soul . When I made it to the trail I picked up my speed again forcing the wind to blow through each strand of hair on my head. I ran that way for half an hour finally making a stop at one of the stretching points.

"You run pretty well. I couldn't keep up with you today."

I heard a voice but it wasn't clear what they said. I pulled one of the earphones out of my ear and searched for the intruder of my quest for solitude. "Excuse me?" My eyes landed on a lean guy. He was cute. Natural hair, brown skin, perfect pearly white teeth, and fit. He had a body of a physical trainer.

"You run pretty well. I've seen you here often just can never keep up with you."

I laughed as I gave him the head to toe assessment. "You're kidding me right. You are obviously in shape. Try another pick-up line why don't you?"

He took a couple steps towards me and laughed. "Miss I was just complimenting you that's all. But ummm yeah enjoy the rest of your run."

I opened my mouth to speak but like the wind, he blew away. I watched him run off in the direction I was going to take and caught myself admiring his strides; among other things.

I shook my head and rolled my eyes. "Cocky ass," I mumbled placing my headphones back into my ears and running back toward my house.

€€€

"Your night was okay?" I asked Janet as I stepped into our adjoined office.

Janet looked up from her desk and nodded her head. "It was great to say the least, yours?"

"Evan and I just went home and to bed. Yay me! So did Kelvin and you do something fun later on?"

Janet laughed and eyed me. "Ugh Ms. Nosey. No, I needed a full body take over and you know there's only one person who does that for me."

I frowned and blew out air. "How did you manage to get rid of Kelvin for Paul missy?"

She shrugged her shoulders and said, "Easy. I told Kelvin good night and messaged Paul to come over. Simple as that. It's not rocket science. You could learn a thing or two from me."

"What? On how to push any man away and just use them as a tool?"

She waved me off, "Girl Kelvin has his women and I don't ask any questions. Men are tools anyway you know."

THE **[image]** I Didn't Say

"You kill me with this alpha female persona you put on."

"It's not a persona Claire. Anyway, why are you in my office bothering me, what's up? Did you have a bad morning?"

I studied her question for a second. Should I tell her on how lonely I was in my own home? How Evan and I seemed more like roommates? Or should I just smile and nod my head as I have grown accustomed to. "No I am fine!" I guess I chose the latter.

Janet raised her eyebrow suspiciously and looked me over. "Trick you're lying, what's up?"

I turned on my heels to walk back to my office. "Nothing." When I heard Janet push herself back from her desk followed by the sounds of her footsteps I began to regret my demeanor.

"Are you okay? Talk to me Claire."

I sat down at my desk and decided to lie.

"I am just suffering from writer's block and boredom. It seems like you have all the fun."

Janet sat on top of my desk and placed her hand on my shoulder.

"It's girl's night out tonight girl. I will not have you holding up on any projects. I am calling the goon squad."

"Your sisters?" I quizzed.

"And my girl Tanya and Jessica from upstairs on the 5th floor. We are about to get it in. Indigo Bar tonight. Wear your tightest dress."

I opened my mouth to protest but she threw up her hand and I knew there was no getting out of it. So I called out, "My tightest huh? I think I can do that."

Denim

I walked on the roof of our studio to admire the scenery of Atlanta. I had them place a deck on the rooftop for when we had networking events.

"Hey babe."

I turned to see Lena walk towards me. I accepted her embrace and gave her a simple kiss on the cheek.

"Hey Lena what's up with you?"

"Dalvin told me you were up here. This is beautiful babe. Good idea to build this."

"Yeah I thought so. So what's up?"

Lena rolled her eyes and her tone changed to that annoying ass buzz that always tend to come out of her mouth when she was nagging me. I needed to drop her ass off back in New York where I met her but she was the best assistant I ever had. "Why do I have to always have to want something? I just wanted to talk," she whined.

I dropped my head and blew out air in an effort to avoid what was obviously about to happen, an unnecessary and confusing conversation. "Nothing Lena." The next assistant I hire must be ugly to make sure I don't fuck her and have to deal with this shit.

"Are you stressed, missing home, what's wrong? It's written all over your face."

What was I supposed to say, that I was missing a woman that I barely knew? Wondering why she hadn't called my phone, needing to hear her voice, desiring to taste her lips again, and that I was mad at myself for being caught up with a stranger. "I'm a little overworked babe. I plan to go relax later on. But I got a few meetings and a studio session in a bit. I will talk to you later." I kissed her on her cheek again and walked away before she could respond.

Making my way down into the office building's hallway I searched for Dalvin. "Yo dog where–" I stopped mid-sentence when I noticed her. My best friend.

"Nitrah!"

She turned around and walked over to me, jumping in my arms. "Hey big baby!" She playfully pushed my head as I greedily hugged her. I held her and squeezed my eyes so tight that I forgot where I was for a moment. "Geesh you sure is happy to see little ole me."

I pulled at her hand and told her to come with me. As we made my way into my office and I shut my door she asked, "Boy what is going on with you?"

Nitrah stood in front of me, folded her arms across her chest, and studied me. She knew me the best out of anyone in the world. I had known her since grade school. She was my high school sweetheart, my first love, and the main reason why my heart is so shut off now. I had messed up any future I would ever have with her but at the end of the day, we were family, we were friends, and we loved each other. She was obviously here visiting me from Texas. She now lived in Houston, where I was staying up until a couple months ago.

"You just caught me off guard. What are you doing here?"

"I am checking in on you."

"Are my niece and nephew here? Your husband? Is Jazzaray here?" I said mentioning her best friend.

"Nope just me. I came to spend time with you." She paused and studied me. "Something is going on here. Your eyes look different."

I looked away from her shyly and asked, "What are you talking about?" She walked over to me and forced me to sit down behind my desk. She took a seat on top of my desk and studied me.

"Who is she? I can see it all over you Denim."

My head jerked in her direction as shock covered my very being. How did she know?

She laughed lightly and asked what I was thinking, "How did I know huh?"

"Yeah, how did you know?"

Nitrah pushed back her long jet black hair behind her ear. I studied her beauty. Nitrah was without a doubt one of the most beautiful women I had ever known. Her chocolate skin seemed endless at times, like its smooth silky appeal went on and on. "In high school and in college you looked that way when you were with me. I hadn't seen it in damn near a decade but I noticed it just now. That look in your eyes. Your mind is racing, your heart is beating irregular. You are in love. I can see it. It's all over you."

I waved her off and said, "Nah, I am just excited about this new project."

She began to laugh hysterically bringing her hand to her chest and nearly falling over. I rolled my eyes and ignored her. "Denim is you trying to lie to me? To the one person that knows everything about you. And I do mean everything."

I eyed her and said, "I don't want to talk about it Nitrah."

She shrugged her shoulders and said, "Fine you don't have to talk about anything. I will be here for a full week bugging the shit out of you. So what's first, you need help on something?"

My smile grew bright. "You know I love you right?"

She leans down and kisses me on the forehead. "Yes baby boy. I love you too. Now let's get some of your work out of the way so that we can go out tonight."

Janet

I grind my hips with my Jamaican friend Tanya, winding all the way down to the floor and back up again as the sounds of "Promise" by Ciara serenaded us. I was in my zone, my vibe was great as I pulled Claire by the hand and forced her to dance on me. She was a shy, sheltered little thing. Always the good one out of the bunch, holding our purses while we went to go get drinks, but not tonight. Tonight she was going to get it in. "Evan who?" I yelled out causing us all to laugh.

Claire bounced her hips so well I noticed a guy looking at her. I walked over to him and yelled in his ear over the music, "Dance with my girl!"

He eyed me, giving me the "are you sure" look. I nodded my head yes and took him by the hand. I announced to the girls, "Ladies this is our new friend." I looked over to Claire. "He wants to dance."

Claire's eyes grew big as if I had just asked her to have sex with the man or something. "Girl please, just dance with the man you don't even have to touch him. Live a little damn," Tanya yelled out. "Look I'll dance with y'all." She grabbed Claire as we all surrounded the one guy and went in.

Claire loosened up after a few songs. She and Tanya had taken over the guy I had brought over. I was tired so when I eyed my sisters sitting at the bar I made my way over to them. My oldest sis, Diamond, was nose deep in some guys face and my baby sis, Nicole, was studying her drink.

"Hey baby girl are you okay?" I asked, taking a seat next to her.

She rolled her eyes. "You know how your sister Diamond can get when she sees a potential cutie." She turned and looked over towards the dance floor. "I see you got your girl Claire to loosen up. Good. She is such a damn square."

I playfully hit her shoulder while I ordered a martini. "Leave my girl alone. Shit, she's one of the last good girls left. Her man just doesn't appreciate her."

"Girl that's all men. Shoot, looks like you're trying to dirty her up like you. You used to be a good girl too Janet, or did you forget?"

I waved her off and laughed, "Yep I forgot." I took a sip of my drink and studied her. "Everything okay with you? I haven't seen you in a couple weeks." I was close to my sisters but after we each relocated here to Atlanta we kind of took on our own lives. Now we were only able to get together a few times a month.

"I'm good; I am a freelance photographer for Juicy Magazine now."

I smiled brightly. "Wow sis! I didn't know they had a division here in Atlanta."

"They just built it. I am pretty excited about it too. Looking to start freelancing for a few more publications too," Nicole added.

I gave her a kiss on the cheek. "Proud of you baby girl. Now if your sis can stop macking maybe we can all toast to your new position."

After hearing me reference her; Diamond said goodbye to her friend and turned to us. "Okay toasting to what now?"

"Your baby sis is freelancing for Juicy." I repeated the news that Nicole had just shared with me.

Diamond screamed and kissed her on the cheek while raising her drink in the air. I laughed and waved off her over the top antics. "What's new with you Diamond?"

"Nothing. Just work and these niggas won't leave a chick alone. You know once they get a taste of Diamond it's all over for them."

THE ~~Shit~~ I Didn't Say

Nicole and I rolled our eyes, "Oh Lord shut up with that please."

Diamond gave me a confused look and pointed. "Janet who is this guy staring at you?"

I followed her eyes and I felt as if my breath left my lungs as my heart began to beat irregularly. "Oh my God. It's him again."

Nicole and Diamond asked in unison, "Who?"

"I'll tell you all about him later. Give me a minute." I hopped off of my seat and walked over to him. "Denim!"

He began to walk out of the VIP section and smiled. "This is beginning to look desperate on your end, so why don't you just ask me out already versus following me around this city."

I laughed and folded my arms across my chest. "What are you doing here?"

"One of my artists is performing tonight."

"Oh so you're here working." He loosened my folded arms and grabbed my hand.

"Not anymore. Come sit with me in VIP. I'll get my security to bring your girls over too."

I turned around and mouth words "I like him" to my sisters hoping that he didn't see.

I followed him into the VIP section and he introduced me to random people in the group. Then he introduced me to his best friend, Dalvin, and Nitrah, a gorgeous woman he called his friend. I eyed her a little longer than I should have. He said she was his friend, but where I came from women and men couldn't be friends.

I waved hello to everyone and took a seat towards the back next to Denim. "Anything you want to drink?"

"Well, I left my drink at the bar. I can get another martini?" Denim signaled for a lady to come here.

"Lena can you go get Janet a martini on the rocks and ask them to bring a large order of wings too." Lena nodded her head okay but not before purposely rolling her eyes at me.

"Another friend?" I asked him after she left.

"No, just my assistant." Denim pushed backwards into his seat and brought his arm over my shoulder. "You look really nice."

I laughed and eyed his arm wrapped around me and said, "Comfortable aren't we?"

He jumped towards the right creating some space between us and hooked his hands together. "Oh my bad I was a tad bit comfortable there."

I laughed and said, "Yeah I wonder why huh."

Denim

"Nothing else compares when I'm caught up in the rapture of you."- Anita Baker

Janet placed her hand on my knee and looked me in the face. "It's fine. I was just highlighting the fact that you were comfortable. See I can do it too." Janet slowly moved in closer to me and cuffed my arm with hers.

I laughed. "You are seriously a different type of woman you know that?"

She leaned down to grab the drink Lena had just placed in front of her and smiled. "So I have been told." She took a sip and then turned to me, "So are you enjoying Atlanta so far?"

"It's cool. Another fake industry circle. Nothing new that I haven't seen before."

"I agree, I try to stay away from all of that." She leaned in towards me and crossed her legs.

"Now look who's getting comfortable," I teased.

She shrugged her shoulders. "What? A big man like yourself is quite comfy so sue me for invading your space." She took a huge swallow of her drink and then laughed. "My sisters are making themselves comfortable over there too."

"Who all came with you anyway?" I said, trying to look over the crowd.

"My sisters Nicole and Diamond, my friends Tanya and Jessica, and my business partner Claire."

He pointed towards Claire who I noticed was taking a drink from Diamond and said, "Yes I saw her with you the other night." He eyed me and smirked, "Have you told her about me?"

I smacked my lips, "I don't even know you!"

"That's the problem you know."

"What Denim?"

I let out an obvious moan when she said my name. "That you do not know me. I love the way you say my name by the way."

"You do?"

"I do!"

There was an obvious pause. Janet's head was pressed up against my shoulder as she looks upward towards me.

"The other night…are we going to pretend it didn't happen?"

Janet dropped her head and took a sip of her drink before rising up to place it back on the table. "I don't know."

"You don't know what?"

Still leaning forward she turns her head back and looks at me. Her eyes had that look again, fearful and sad. I stood up and grabbed her hand. I motioned for my security D Boy to follow us out onto the balcony. Janet frantically looked at me and all around us. I told her sisters and friends that she would be right back and that we were headed towards the balcony.

"What are you doing?" Janet asked.

"We should talk. Without the music, without the crowd of people, without distractions. I finally got a chance to pull you away."

"Again?" She challenged.

"Again!"

"What is it that you want to know Denim?"

I leaned up against the railing and began to overlook the night's darkness. Then I studied her.

"Don't look at me like that Denim," she begged.

"Like what?"

"Just like that!"

"Like I want you? Like I need you?" Shocked at what I had just said, she turned her head and looked at me.

"Don't talk like that."

THE 📖 I Didn't Say

I threw my hands in the air. "It's been what, a little over a week and I can't get you out of my head. Every second, every moment, everything reminds me of you. It reminds me of you Janet." I cupped her chin, forcing her to look at me.

Her eyes were that of a small child, fearful and vulnerable. I kissed her lips and allowed us to connect once more until she pulled away. "Don't!"

"You feel that too Janet. I know you do. I haven't felt this since…" My voice trailed off. "What is this?"

Janet dropped her head into her hands and said, "I don't know what this is Denim. I can't say it."

"Come with me tonight Janet. Just spend some time with me."

Janet took steps backwards. "I can't do that. I…I…I would kiss you. And I can't kiss you."

I walked over to her and grabbed her shoulders. "Why not Janet, why?"

She threw her head backwards to look up to me and I could see the fear and sadness in her eyes. "I just can't."

"Is there someone else?" I asked.

"No," she shot back.

"When then? I won't stop Janet. The feeling you give me is…I can't even explain it. It's like I feel you when you're not even with me. I can hear you. I can see you. I am connected to you and I don't know why."

She dropped her head down and whispered, "Yeah, I know!"

"You know?"

She angrily threw her head up and looked at me, "Yes I know. I feel it too okay!" She raised her hand and pushed me backwards. "Look please give me time. Give me space. I just need to think."

"Time. How much time?"

"Denim I do not know."

She turned on her heels and walked back into the club. I could see she was telling her friends that she was leaving. Only Claire got up to go with her. My head of security walked over to me and placed his hand on my shoulder.

"Fight for her dog. I ain't ever seen you this in love."

I frowned at him. "In love?"

"Yeah dog you love that woman. Only a man in love pleads like that."

I waved him off and told him to pull my car around. I wasn't going to stay to listen to my artist. I needed to get away. "And tell Nitrah to bring her ass on."

€€€

I was neck deep in my marble Jacuzzi tub in my high-rise condo in Buckhead. Nitrah had put some relaxing oils in my tub and lit candles around the room. I appreciated the touch but was annoyed with the sweet ambiance of it all. It reminded me that I wanted Janet there with me.

I heard a knock on the door and then Nitrah's voice. "Baby boy are you okay?"

"Yeah!" I called back.

I reached for my phone that sat on the marble counter next to my tub and searched for Janet's name. I text: hey.

I waited the longest five minutes I had ever experienced when she finally responded with: hi!

Denim: what are you doing?

Janet: Lying in my bed listening to my Pandora

Denim: Oh yeah what station?

Janet: Luther Vandross but of course. That man can blow.

Denim: My favorite is the Raheem Devaughn channel

Janet: What would a big softy like you know about Raheem Devaughn?

Denim: LOL wouldn't you like to know? I've cut some music with the man before

Janet: No way

Denim: Yes way

THE ~~SH!T~~ I Didn't Say

Janet: Don't think that you are all that Mr. Overton

Denim: Oh but I am lol. Ms. Jamison Aye...

Janet: Yes????

Denim: Once I get out of this tub can I call you?

Janet: You want to cupcake on the phone I see?

Denim: I just want to hear your voice that's all

Janet: I'm gonna hop in the shower give me thirty minutes, cool?

Denim: Cool

I bathed and hopped out of the tub, wrapping one of my large plush towels around my waist. I marched around the room and blew out the candles and then made my way into my bedroom. For once I was in a bed alone. No women. No entourage was roaming through my house. No interruptions.

I called Janet and we talked on the phone for hours. I had never done that before.

Claire

I threw my shoes across the living floor and stumbled in planting myself on the couch. I had a huge headache but thank God Janet had been my ride tonight. The lights being turned on forced me to pay attention to my surroundings. That's when I noticed Evan seated on the couch across from me.

"Oh hey!" I said.

"Woman it's two in the morning. Do you want to tell me why you are getting home at two in the morning and why your phone is going to voicemail?"

"You're home?" I asked ignoring his question. "Surprised." I rose up from my seat and made my way to the stairs.

"Woman did you hear me?"

"Yeah I did. Did you hear me?"

"I can come home when I damn well please and your ass is supposed to be here when I get here."

I rolled my eyes and laughed. "Negro who are you now; Ike Turner, a Mr. Mike Tyson wannabe? I went out with my friends. Simple." I began my walk up the stairs as I heard Evan prance behind me.

"Where were you Claire?"

I jerked around and yelled, "We went dancing damn! What is the big deal? I never go out anyway."

"Let me smell you!"

"What?" I screamed back, halfway disgusted. What did he say?

Evan pulled at my arm and forced me to walk faster up the stairs. I yelled at him asking what he was doing but he wasn't listening to anything I was saying. He kept chanting "I'm going to see for myself."

In our room he flicked on the light and told me to walk over to the bed. I stared at the bed and then towards him. "What?"

"Walk over to the bed Claire or I will walk you over myself," he demanded. I stood planted in the same spot when he began to angrily march towards me pushing me backwards.

"What are you doing? Stop!" I screamed out as his forceful hands pinned on my arms became unbearable. He held them so tight that I could no longer feel my hands. He continued pushing me towards the bed and yelling at me to lie down. "For what?"

"I'm really not going to ask you again Claire. You can make this easy or you can make this hard."

I studied my husband's face. There was a stranger in my house and it was evident that he was not himself at this moment. But how could I fight him? How could I resist him forcing me to lie on the bed like some animal so that he can check my privates?

I closed my eyes as I slowly pulled down my panties one leg at a time. I felt that time was standing still as I experienced the biggest violation of my life.

"Lie down." He demanded.

I couldn't believe I was being forced to do such a thing. I can do this. I can get through this.

I lay back flat on the bed and closed my eyes. I could feel him over me he leans down and smells my neck, my fingers, and then my mouth. "Your mouth stinks," he blurts out. His voice was empty and cold. My lips began to quiver as the pain of it all was beginning to take over my mind.

I flinch at his touch. For the first time in my life, Evan's touch felt like a violation. The feeling caused my skin to burn and my stomach to churn in knots. "Hurry up!" I screamed in anger.

He lifts my legs and forces them open. I could feel him towering over me and then he did the unthinkable, he pushed his fingers inside of me. I jumped up and away. "Get the fuck away from me you son of a bitch. Dirty ass motherfucker. I will kill you. Get your fucking hands off of me," I cried.

Evan raised his hands as if was he were surrendering. "Yeah you're clean. I just had to make sure."

"Make sure what? That I wasn't fucking someone else like you. Fuck you Evan! Get the hell out of my way." I rushed into our bathroom, ripped my clothes off of me, and threw myself into our shower. I fell to my knees and cried like a baby. I cried so hard that my throat tightened up so making it hard to breathe.

I didn't take time to wash up. I rushed out of the shower, dried off, and went into my closet and threw on some clothes. I threw whatever I could manage to grab into a bag and placed on my runner's shoes. I rushed out of my room and down the stairs realizing Evan must be in his man cave. Perfect!

He must have heard the jingling of my keys when I grabbed them because he called my name. I frantically ran out the front door not even closing the door behind me. I pressed unlock on my car doors and jumped in. When I got behind the wheel I could see Evan running out the house. I screamed out nervously, locking my doors and cranking the car. I pulled out so quick the tires screeched loudly awakening the entire neighborhood.

I didn't look back to see if he was following me. I just drove to the only place I knew that I could go.

Janet

He thought he was slick. But I wasn't falling for it. He was a smooth talker, but I knew I was quoting that to myself to deny that I liked him. I mean I really liked him. I began to think about my Head Hunter. I needed him right now in the worst way so that he could distract me from Denim. I glanced at my bedside clock and it read a little after four in the morning. I had been on the phone now for three hours.

Wait. Three hours? What the hell were we even talking about? "Wait you played soccer as a kid, what did they use your head?" I laughed out. I had no idea that we had covered so much ground. Talking to him was easy, it was familiar, it was like...normal. Yeah that's the feeling. This felt normal.

"Don't front you know you like my head!" Denim shot back. I couldn't help but laugh as he attempted to insinuate a sexual joke. He was so corny.

"What's the best part about being you?" I asked him. He paused for a minute and repeated my question. "Yeah what do you enjoy the most about your life?"

"I've never been asked those questions before. I guess the fact that I am living out my dream you know. I was always the one who threw together the high school house parties. I would DJ every small gathering, and then it got bigger and bigger until the city knew me. I just wanted to make people dance to my beats that's all."

"Sounds like you accomplished a lot Mr. Overton."

"Sounds like you did too Ms. Jamison. Tell me, what's the best part about being you?"

I should have known he was going to throw that question back at me. "Hmmm the best part huh? Well I get to lie and not be frowned upon," I laughed.

"Huh?" He quizzed.

I sat straight up in my bed as I became more engrossed in our conversation. "I used to always have these stories in my head. And I would always force a dream, like a vision. And then one day I decided to write it out. I let the characters talk and I created lives. I created drama. I created love. None of it was true stuff but it gave me life. To create lives on paper gave me life. So yeah I am lying so to speak because they aren't real."

"Now when you break it down like that, the lying part, that all makes sense. I like that."

"I bet you do. Anyway don't you have some work to do or something?"

"Oh you must be trying to rush me off the phone now. It's cool, it's cool, I'll move over for now," Denim laughed out.

"No, I'm simply saying it's over three hours on the phone now. I didn't take you as the phone talking type. I know I'm not."

"Why aren't you?"

I blew out hot air and became annoyed with where this conversation was going. "I just don't talk on the phone that's all."

"Why not?" He pressed the question again.

I fell backwards onto my pillows and blew out air again. "Why what?"

"Why don't you talk on the phone Janet? You heard me." Denim's voice has been light and friendly most of our conversation but now it was serious, low, and stern.

"Because having conversations builds feelings."

"Hmmm and you don't desire to build feelings?"

"No Denim, I do not desire to build feelings. I can keep it moving very easily."

"Is that so?"

I opened my mouth to respond when I heard knocking on my door. I jerked upward and whispered, "Who the hell is banging on my door like that?"

THE I Didn't Say

"Are you okay?" Denim asked.

"Hold on!" I pulled my phone off of my ear and text him my address. "I just text you my address. If this is trouble at my front door you better call 911."

"Okay, okay I got it. I am listening though. Go see what's up. What do you have in your hand?"

"My hand?"

"Yeah for protection."

"My gun. I live alone so of course I own one."

"Well shit, call 911 for what Ms. Kill Bill!"

I shushed him as I made my way to my front door and made a small viewing hole through my curtains. I saw Claire's car in my driveway. "Claire!"

I unlocked my door and she rushed in. "I need to stay with you tonight." I closed and locked the door behind me.

"Denim it's Claire. Everything is fine. I will call you back, okay?"

"Okay but if I don't hear from you by the am I am using this address."

I laughed and said okay as I hung up. I walked over to Claire who was now stretched across my couch. I pulled at her to sit up but she refused and she looked horrible.

"Claire what in the world is going on? Why do you look like this? Let me call your husband."

Claire jumped up and yelled, "No don't call him!"

Her eyes grew big and her breathing became erratic. I recognize the fear. What in the hell did this man do to her? Oh hell nah I will have to beat his ass.

"Okay we won't call him but let's get you changed and comfortable. You can sleep in the Queen guest room." I led her to the room grabbing some wash cloths and towels in the process and placing them in the guest bath. "Wash up Claire and get some rest we can talk about it tomorrow or not, okay?"

She nodded her head, holding back tears as I closed the door for her to shower.

I walked back into my living room and looked out the blinds. "I know that man will come here looking for her and when he does my gun is ready."

Denim

"I believe that every single event in life that happens is an opportunity for you to choose love over fear," Nitrah said, walking into my kitchen heading straight for the food I had my chef prepare.

"Don't start this morning."

"I just finished watching Life Class with Oprah Winfrey. She quoted that and it just stuck in my head. I thought of you when she said it."

I ignored her, dropping more bites of my eggs into my mouth. "Good morning to you too. I had something made for you. It's in the microwave."

"Oooo I can get use to this D, so what are we doing today?" Nitrah said, hopping on the barstool next to me as she began to indulge in her food.

I looked at my watch it read eight am. I was going to give Janet thirty more minutes before I actually acted out my threat to show up at her house. "Going into the office for a few hours to check on Dalvin then we can go downtown and do whatever you want."

"How about you give me that black card to go shopping and you go out with the lady you spent all night talking to."

I eyed her in shock. "Huh?"

"Dude I heard you laughing loud as hell last night. Laughing D, you were laughing. I think I like her. She was the one at the club last night huh?"

I nodded my head yes. "What did you think of her?"

"She's a beauty, a little like me if I say so myself."

I rolled my eyes. "You just did."

"Yeah go out with her, I am rooting for this one here. When did you two meet anyway? You have never mentioned her at all."

"It was just last week, well almost two weeks now."

Nitrah dropped her fork and stared at me. "Last week. You mean to tell me you met her last week?"

I nodded my head yes.

"Dude but you two seem like y'all knew each other, you seemed seasoned if you asked me. Weird!"

"Yeah weird." I opened my wallet and dropped my card on the counter. "Don't do too much damage Nitrah. I will kick your ass."

Grabbing the card off the table and placing it in her bra she laughed and said, "Negro you ain't gonna kick shit. Thanks though."

I waved her off grabbing my cell phone. I text Janet, "I will see you today!" She replied back five minutes later. Ok! And my smile never left my face.

Claire

"Did Evan come by here?" I asked Janet making my way into her kitchen.

"No, but that's because I told him that I was strapped and ready."

"You called him?"

"Yes, but he didn't tell me what happened. I didn't ask, you will tell me if you want me to know." Janet walked into her room. I followed behind her and noticed she had clothes draped across her bed.

"Where are you going?"

"I think on a date!" Janet glowed as her smile spread wide. I studied her and then I knew.

"The guy from the lounge that night. You're going out with him."

She turned and looked at me scrunching her nose as if something was stinky. "Why would you say him of all people?"

"Because of your smile, you don't smile like that with any of the other ones but you smiled like that on that night."

"Hmmmm I guess so huh? Yeah, I am going out with him. He didn't tell me where though."

"Must be nice." I plopped down on her bed and buried my face in her pillow.

"Ugh girl do not be messing up my sheets. Are you going to tell me what happened or what?"

"I'll rather not, not right now. It wasn't that bad we just had an argument," I said, burying my face further into her pillow.

Janet smacked her lips in disbelief and announced, "If he fucked with you I will fuck him up. I can't stand men. They are all the same anyway."

I waved her off. "I'll be going home in a bit. I already did text him but of course he's gone off to work. Are you going into the office today?"

"To be honest because I don't know what he has planned so probably not. But definitely tomorrow because I have two meetings set up."

I rose up from her bed, walked over to her, and hugged her. "Enjoy your date you deserve it. I get tired of you using these men because of what Desmond did."

She put up her hand and shushed me, "Do not mention Desmond in my house. I am good Claire I promise you. I don't need love and apparently neither do you."

She kissed me on my cheek and went into her bathroom to wash up and get dressed. I followed her process and was dressed and out of her home in thirty minutes. I didn't want to go back home but I have never been one to walk away so easily. I married Evan because I loved him and I was certain we could get better.

€€€

I walked into my home quiet as kept and searching the premises. He wasn't here. I walked up the stairs and into my room and dropped my bag. I looked at my bed. Flashbacks of last night came rushing to the surface. I turned my head angrily and rushed into my closet. I picked out my running gear, placed it on, and I was out the front door once more.

I felt at home again when the Spring air began to dance on my flesh. I pointed my head towards the sky and embraced the suns beams. I opened my mouth slightly to steady my breathing. Once entering the lake's trail I put more speed into my strides. I think I was running faster today. Either that or I just felt like I was floating.

I closed my eyes and imagined that I was invisible when I collided and fell backwards onto the ground. "Ahhh!" I yelled out in pain as my ass hit the hard pavement. I realized I had run into a person when I noticed them reach down to help me up.

"Running like the wind today, huh?"

That voice. I looked up and realized it was him again. The guy I insulted when I insinuated that he was flirting. I put my hand into his as I stood up and began to brush off my pants. "Sorry and thanks."

"Are you okay?" He asked.

"I'll be fine." I said, finally taking my attention off of my pants and back towards him.

"Lewis!"

I raised my hand over my face to block the sun from my eyes and said, "Huh?"

"I'm Lewis." He extended his hand again for me to shake it. I did.

"Claire."

"Let's see if I can keep up with you now that you have this wounded leg," he laughed.

I smiled slightly and made a mental note not to insult him again. "Wounded. No honey I can still run circles around you."

He raised an eyebrow and curiously bit his lips. "Are you certain of that?" I felt a sudden jolt in my midsection that made me look downward to see if anything jumped up and bit me.

I felt a tingling sensation and realized my kitty was a little more than excited. Oh my goodness did this man just make my kitty jump? "Yeah I am certain."

Lewis looked at me with concern. "Is it your leg?"

Hell no it ain't my leg and I can't tell you what it is. I became bashful wanting the feeling in between my legs to subside. But it wasn't working with me just standing here and staring at this God forsaken fine ass man in the face.

"Let's run. Ready?" I took off like the wind again and I could hear Lewis a couple steps behind me until we were side by side.

Our strides matched perfectly and when he suggested we run over to the Smoothie King a mile away I obliged his offer. I mean I didn't have anything else to do anyway.

Denim

I sat across from Janet at a tapas bar. Live music was playing, the ambiance was romantic, and the dim room complimented her complexion. I scooted my seat closer to her. "You look nice."

She blushed and then eyed my seat, "Negro why are you scooting closer to me?"

"It's cold over there," I whined.

"Cold? It's what; three inches from me?"

"That's three inches too far." I kissed her bare shoulder and studied her. She rolled her eyes and laughed.

"Get out of my face Denim."

I raised up my hands in surrender. "Fine, fine, have it your way missy. So what are you ordering?"

"Grilled octopus perhaps?" I gave her a disgusted look as she laughed out. "Ever had calamari?"

I shrugged my shoulders. "Yeah and?" She stared at me blankly. "No way, that can't be."

" No" She laughed. "But you get my point." "Okay, okay let's do some soups and some grilled shrimp to start off, cool with you?"

"Cool with me," I said, taking a sip of my brown liquor. "You come here often?"

"Just to listen to the music and eat a little seafood. It's one of my favorite places. Figured I'll bring you here, bring you into my world a little bit."

"It's cool but where are the juke joints, the hole in the walls, the mom and pop joints?"

Janet turned in her chair and said, "Oh I'll have to ask one of my gay friends who is from here. It's plenty, I just don't know any personally. You know I'm not from here. But that's what you want? Hmmm."

"Hmmm what woman?" I challenged her.

"I'm just saying you are a man of a certain class now and you want to eat at a hole in the wall."

"Doesn't matter how deep my pockets get Janet I still want to eat good food," I laughed.

"I see I underestimated you. That's kind of attractive."

I wrapped my arms around her waist and gave her a playful squeeze. "Oh now I'm attractive. Yes! I moved up in rank."

"Ha ha not funny. Back up off me."

"Dang you are mean." I threw a napkin playfully at her face. She pulled it off and laughed with her mouth hung open.

I heard a woman walk up behind us and ask, "Excuse me, but you're DJ Denim O right?"

I wanted to bury my face in my menu and ignore her. But Janet turned to her and said, "He's a little under the weather, but what can I do for you."

"Oh we just wanted a picture," she said.

Janet placed her hand on my shoulder and whispered, "Babe can they get a picture? It'll only take five seconds."

I eyed her and smiled. Often times when I was with other women, if someone asked for a picture or an autograph they grew jealous. But not her, she seemed comfortable with who I was. She seemed like a pro at getting people in and out of your space. I nodded my head without saying a word and turned to the ladies. I got in between them as Janet took the pic and just as simple as that; they were out of our space. I turned and looked at her, "Babe?"

"That was good huh?" She laughed taking a sip of her tea.

"I think I like you just a little bit more."

"Oh so you like me huh?"

"You aight!"

THE 🎵 I Didn't Say

She threw her head back and laughed again, "You're funny DJ Denim O. I mean I haven't even gotten a picture yet with Mr. Famous."

"That's because I plan to give you more than just a picture." I stared at Janet with just as much desire in my eyes as she did. From her smile, her laugh, to her jokes, and the easy flow of our conversations I wanted her in the worst way. "Do you remember the bathroom?"

Janet dropped her head shyly and turned her attention back to her drink. "Yeah I remember. And?"

"I want that again." I didn't want to jump around my point. I felt I had Janet in a moment that was rare. I could sense a lot of resistance with her and for that reason I tried to come in easy. But damn was I yearning for another kiss. Just one.

"That? What was that?" Janet asked.

"The kiss of my life," I whispered.

She jerked her head towards me and mouthed, "What?"

"You heard me."

"I don't need to be wooed by your words Denim. I am not like these groupies running around here."

"That you are not. And I am not wooing you with my words. I don't have to because I know you believe me."

"Believe you? What is this; sweet talk Janet to death session?" She rolled her eyes and took a sip of her tea again.

"You're fighting me? Why?" She grew quiet and I didn't press the issue. I just sat back and watched her and she knew I was watching her too.

"Like dude really; you can't focus on your plate instead of me?" She blurted after the waitress came and sat our food down in front of us.

"What's up Janet?"

"Nothing, just hungry."

"Okay let's eat and then we can just enjoy the rest of the night."

I decided to change the subject and not pressure her. Janet shook her head okay as she turned her attention to the band. I could see the tension in her shoulders as she looked onward. Something bothered her and I felt it was my job to make it okay. But I could already tell that it was going to be like Fort Knox to bring her walls down.

Janet

I yelled at Diamond to hurry her slow ass up. I had just about thirty minutes to get everything ready before he walked through the door and I was not going to allow her to mess this up. Thirty days. I had planned this surprise for thirty days and it was finally the day. I was nervous. I felt like my own breath was going to suffocate me with the way I was breathing.

"Move your ass Diamond!"

"Look trick don't be yelling at me like I am your damn servant. Nobody told your ass to get all these damn flowers anyway! And don't expect me to show up tomorrow to clean up this shit. Hire someone next time!" Diamond said, tossing rose petals on the floor.

"Whatever, whatever, whatever. Get it done." I ran into my room frantically finding the stockings and negligee I planned to wear when he walked through that door.

"Are you almost done?" I heard her call out.

"Yes give me five minutes."

I rushed into my bathroom and glanced at the clock. He would be in his limo right now on his way home. Just leaving the spa I had him sent to. Just when I was about to tell Diamond she could leave we heard a knock on the door.

"I'll get it!" Diamond called out. "Sis you are gonna want to come here."

I marched into the living room and curiously looked at her. She stood in front of the doorway and I walked over to see who was on the other side. I didn't recognize him. "Yes?"

"Are you Janet Jamison?"

I walked over to him and nodded my head. "Yes I am, you're the driver right? What are you doing here?"

"We waited on Mr. Howard until about twenty minutes ago. He wasn't at the location you gave us. Here is the return on your tip monies but we will have to charge you for the hours we spent waiting. Good day ma'am."

I was totally confused. With my mouth dropped and looked over to Diamond who looked just as confused as I. "Where the fuck is Desmond if he wasn't at work?" She asked.

I wanted to know the same thing. It had been hours since he was supposed to get off and experience the surprise I had planned for him. I knew to catch him on Thursday nights before he headed out with drinks with his fellas. I would surprise him with a stretch limo to pick him up take him to a spa downtown. Then he would be driven to a men's store to get a new tailored suit and then home to me, where I had a chef cook us a meal, rose petals were everywhere, and I was going to perform a dance I learned over the course of a month at the Lily Jazz Studio.

I picked up my cell phone and called him but his phone was going to voicemail . He had been off for four hours now. There was no excuse.

"This is some bull shit!" Diamond announced. "I placed all those roses on the floor so his ass is seeing this shit tonight."

I waved her off and text his phone. No response. I text his brother. No response. "What the hell is going on?" I called his best friend , Isaac. He picked up.

"What's going on? Where is Desmond?"

"Janet you should get to Kennestone Hospital ASAP. No one wanted to call you but I think it's only right that you know."

"Know what?" I asked him.

"Just get here and tell the receptionist you're looking for Desmond."

The phone went dead and I repeated what he said to me to Diamond.

"Something fishy is going on? I am going with you. Sounds like you may need back up," Diamond said.

THE [illegible] I Didn't Say

I changed my clothes and hopped into my car headed straight to the hospital. I kept texting Desmond along the way but still got no response. When we got there. Diamond and I marched into the ER and made our way to the receptionist's desk when I heard someone call my name. I turned to see it was Isaac.

I gave him a soft hug and waited for him to tell me what was up. "Desmond was in an accident."

"An accident?" Diamond yelled over me.

"What kind of accident are you talking about?"

He led us past the ER doors and we walked a few hallways when he began to speak again. "I thought it was only right to tell you but what you are about to find out you should have heard from Desmond but he isn't conscious right now."

I looked at him with confusion when Diamond blurted, "Dude you are making no sense. Where is he?"

He pointed towards a patient door. Placing my hand on it, I slowly pushed it open and noticed a few of Desmond's friends and family here. There he laid in the bed as if he was sleeping but he had a tube down his throat.

"What happened?"

I could see the people in the room whispering and carrying on but no one answered me. Diamond raised her hand and said, "Obviously we are missing something. Why wasn't my sister called to see about her man. Why is everyone looking at us like we are not supposed to be here?"

His best friend walked over to me and said, "Desmond got married two weeks ago. His wife died in the car accident."

I jerked my head to look at him; the tears in my eyes were evidence of my pain and confusion. "Married? But we have been together for five years. We live together. We came here from Texas together and you're telling me he got married and all of you knew. I have been y'all family for five years and no one told me?"

"This is some straight up bullshit and if that negro wasn't lying up in that hospital bed right now I would beat his ass. He

50

better not be faking." Diamond yelled. I fell backwards into his Isaac arms and pushed away from him angrily.

I looked at Desmond lying in the hospital bed and grew madder by the second. He laid there lifeless. The woman he had married was dead but I felt nothing for him. I didn't feel sorry. I felt betrayal. Was I wrong for feeling this way?

"Let's go," I called out to Diamond. I turned to Isaac. "I hope he makes it. You can come get all of his things starting tomorrow or they will be in the trash."

The story of Desmond Howard is why I am the way I am today. A maneater. I never spoke to him after the fact and because of that this chapter in my life still isn't complete...

Back to present day….

Denim

I walked into my wine cellar and grabbed the finest red wine that I had. After texting Nitrah to not show up any time soon I sent everyone who worked for me home and now I had my place to myself. It was sad to say that being in my condo alone was weird but it was. There was always someone here, cleaning, cooking, giving me my schedule, or working. But lately I had been taking some down time mainly because Nitrah was forcing me to.

"Red wine right?" I asked Janet as I made my way back into the living room. She nodded her head yes. I watched her cup her feet underneath her as she grabbed one of my couch pillows and snuggled against it. "Did you want something to snack on babe?"

"No, I'm good," she called out.

I walked in, handed her the glass, and studied her. She asked, "You like to stare don't you?"

"At you? Well of course."

"You're a smooth talker I tell ya. Anyone ever told you that?"

"Maybe one or two people once upon a time," I laughed, taking a sip of my wine.

"Figures." Janet took a gulp of her wine and I studied her. Her shell was so hard now for some reason. Her face was still the same. Beautiful, innocent looking, her almond shaped chin trailed to her button shaped nose, and I loved everything about her. Even this so called attitude she would put on.

"You're harder now, you know that right?"

"Harder?"

I scooted closer to her placing my glass on the table in front of us and repeated myself. "Why are you single?"

"Why am I single?"

"You heard me Janet. Tell me why."

She paused, taking her attention away from me and towards the skyline views outside my window. "I choose to be. I don't do this."

"What?"

"This!" She said, pointing towards the ground.

"Me?"

"Yeah, you are a part of this."

"And what is this Janet because I do not know. I have been trying to figure it out too."

"I don't know. I just know that it's not normal. I don't think about guys the next day. I don't get on the phone and talk for hours. I don't do dates."

I pushed back from her shocked at her proclamation. "You sound like a guy. You sound like me."

"You do the same thing?" Her focus was now directly on me. We sat there nearly nose to nose speaking as if we were in a room full of people and had to whisper.

"I do that."

"Why? Tell me why?"

"I don't think you want to know Janet. I mean I don't usually share my thoughts with anyone. I mean no one gets in here." I pointed towards my chest and signaled towards my heart.

"But am I? Am I there?" When I didn't answer her she brushed her hands across my ear to my cheek and then leaned down and kissed my nose. "Tell me and I will tell you. You don't have to go into details. Just a broad reason as to why no one gets this."

"I was in love once. The damage I created couldn't be reversed. In turn, she became me; she had become the one that broke my heart along with a few others. She managed to change though; be happy, have kids, and get married. But to this day we are the best of friends."

"Nitrah?" She asked. I nodded my head yes.

"I have been the same since high school. I idolize women. Love everything about them."

"So you're a whore?"

"So to speak." We laughed. "Now it's your turn."

Janet paused and blew out her breath. She readjusted her seating and again looked away from me as if she was shy. "I wasn't a hoe. I wasn't a liar. I wasn't a cheater. I was none of that."

"But that was done to you?"

"Yes! It's easier not to love someone. No one gets hurt, you know? So that's the motto I live by now. Don't get attached. No sleepovers. No conversations. Nothing."

"Nothing?"

"A random fuck yeah, but nothing more."

"Has that been working for you?"

"It was!" She turned and looked at me. She started to speak but then changed her mind. "Nothing."

"Don't shy away when you speak to me Janet. I won't bite. I promise."

"You probably will." She laughed. Then there was an awkward silence. "Then this. It's like I met you and something within me said finally there you are."

"This is crazy." I pushed away and sat back on my side of the couch and joked, "You aren't even all that."

Janet launched a pillow at my head. I reacted as if I was a wounded child. Laughing she leans over towards me and purrs, "I'm sorry."

I grabbed her by the arms and pulled her into me forcing her to lie down on my chest. "I will try my best not to hurt you Janet. I just want to get to know you."

"You promise," she replied, burying her face into my hardened chest. I squeezed her tightly and I made her a promise. "No strings?" She asked.

"No strings," I replied.

Janet

Yawning, I slowly peek out of my left eye to examine my surroundings. I'm still in the living room. I begin to recalculate my last memories. We had fallen asleep on his couch talking. I was still on top of him, lying on him as if I was his woman.

I shivered at the thought of titles and pushed my head upward as I forced my eyes to open some more. He was in a dead sleep. His face was stiff and expressionless yet he looked so handsome. His full lips were pressed together and I could see the roaming of his eyeballs move underneath his lids.

I moved slowly, rubbing my hand up his chest and then across his chin. I touched his cheeks, then his ears and admired him. My heart felt like it double in size as my chest tightened and my stomach began to churn. I grunted in agony and tried to adjust how I was laying. Every time I looked at him I got this feeling. I remembered this feeling. The feeling Desmond used to give me.

When I turned my head to look back at him, his eyes were partly open. The first fear was accepting his dare to stare head on but I went in anyway. I took in his aura. I listened to the pace of his breathing and our eyes focused in on each other. The feeling I felt at this very moment was perfect. It was as if it was designed specifically to cause me to fall for this man. To be drawn into his soul breath by breath. Kiss him. No, don't kiss him. Do it now Janet.

I hadn't kissed him since that night in the bathroom. The one time where it felt perfect. I was burning inside to kiss this man. I was yearning to feel myself connect to him and I had never wanted this from anyone before. I had only loved once. Just once and that one person broke my heart.

Denim began to rub my arms as if he wanted to warm me up. "You are beautiful," he whispered. I smiled. I bashfully dropped my head when he grabbed my chin and pushed my face back upward. He pulled me up and he did it again. He made me forget that any other kiss I had ever had happened. This kiss was the kiss of all kisses. My lips on top of his, my moans dancing in the air along with his, the mist in my eyes now became passionate tears.

I hungrily grabbed his face and gave all of myself to him. "I love you." He whispered in between kisses. Our kiss stood still. Our breathing was heavy, our eyes were dilated with passion, and my heart was beating rapidly.

"I love you too," I cried out. Did I just tell him that I loved him? Did I just say that? I didn't wait to answer myself; instead, I fell back into Denim's kisses. I fell back into his arms and into his embrace. I loved this feeling. Yes, I think did actually love him.

Denim pushed upward forcing me to rise as our kiss stayed connected. Turning me over on my back he towers over me. I moaned out as I felt the intense pressure of my kitty begin to rise. I pushed my groin into his pelvis as he pushed downward. My hip bone was connected to his hip bone. Our hearts were beating as one. I could feel perspiration seep through my pores and through my clothing. The dampness was evidence that I was sweating out my desire for him.

"Babe…" He moaned as he grabbed and squeezed my body inch by inch.

"Yes?" I cried out squirming underneath him. I didn't protest as I felt his hands come to my waistline pushing my shorts downward. Two fingers on my zipper. Zips down. Opens the flap. Push down. Raise your hips. Slide them down. Lay back and relax. Legs widen.

Denim pushed his mouth into mine as he takes his hands to his pants. Belt buckle. Hole by hole pulls open. Zipper is up. Push it down. Rises up and slides pants down. Boxers. Eliminate those. My head turned to meet his warrior and boy was he ready for war. Denim's dick was beautiful. The right shade of dark and the cutest pink head. It was smooth, as if baby oil had been rubbed all over it. Long, thick, and the vein that was pulsating right down the middle jerked.

"Oh my goodness," I whispered.

Denim came back toward me and towered over me. I widen my legs to accept him and kissed him once more. Our eyes focused in on one another and in one swift move he slides inside of me causing my breath to leave my lungs.

Denim moaned and buried his face into my neck and wrapped his arms around my body. The tears ran heavily down my face hitting the sofa cushions as the passion I felt within my soul became the best moment of my life. I loved him. I had loved Denim even before I knew I did.

Claire

I sat in my home office trying to work. I had been staring at the screen when I heard the front door open. My heart jumped. It was late. Nine at night, I didn't expect to actually see Evan this early.

"Babe!" He called out.

His voice was light and sweet. It made me want to vomit. "What?" I replied.

He walked into my office causally with the corniest smile on his face. "Hey babe how was your day?" He walked over and attempted to kiss me on my cheek and I jerked back. I didn't want him to touch me. I had never felt violated in my entire life and I would have never thought in a million years that my husband would be the person to make me feel that way.

Evan stared at me. His corny smile now gone and was replaced with a look of embarrassment. He placed his hands in his pockets and simply said, "I'm sorry."

I pushed back from my desk and smirked, "Sorry isn't good enough." I walked the opposite direction around my desk and headed towards the living room but before I walked out of my office completely I turned on my heels and eyed him. "Violate me again and it's your life. I promise you on that." I didn't wait for him to reply as I made my way up the stairs.

I think my newfound boldness had much to do with my day with Lewis, my running buddy. I liked how I felt when I was with him. No, he hadn't flirted with me, maybe because my wedding ring served as a repellant, but he was nice. He was friendly and I was going to go running with him again.

I marched into my bedroom and found some comfortable jammies to put on. Nothing too cute. Nothing to give Evan the impression that we were about to do anything. I just wanted to sleep. I wanted to feel like a Queen in her own home and I did when I pulled back the sheets to lay on the very spot my husband violated me. I had taken back my own power. I lay there for a moment before I got up and headed back downstairs. Evan needed a taste of his own medicine.

€€€

I walked into the office to see Janet pounding away on those keyboards. When she noticed me she stopped and gave me her full attention. "I was wondering what happened to you since you left my house. Everything good?"

I smiled brightly. "Everything is good girl, Evan and I just had a fight, that's all. But things are good. I am slowly gaining back some control in our marriage. What about you?"

"I'm focused on knocking out ten thousand words today before we head out to this networking event tonight."

"The Jade Magazine social is tonight? Ugh here we go again," I whined.

"Yes here we go again." I looked over to Janet who now had turned her focus back to her writing and noticed she looked different.

"Wait something is up with you. Is it Mr. Denim perhaps?" I laughed marching in and sitting down on top of her desk.

"Well maybe it is. But we're just getting to know each other for now."

I moaned, "Yeah okay whatever. Hold your tongue if you must. But I am sure you'll be skipping and singing around here soon enough. That'll tell me enough. Is he gonna be your date tonight?"

"No, he is going to the studio tonight catching up on some work. But I may see him afterwards. But let me get this word count up before tonight and you too ma'am."

59

THE ▨ I Didn't Say

"Alright don't pressure me Ms. Imallinlove." I laughed as she waved me off proclaiming she wasn't in love. I wasn't any fool. I knew love when I saw it.

Janet

I walked into the upscale lounge side by side with Claire and Nicole. The ambiance was bright as the golden fixtures were dazzling and reflecting off of the ceiling lights.

"This is a nice setting," Claire said over the music.

I had a great vibe going on not because of last night with Denim. Okay, okay maybe that's why. But the DJ was playing that classic 90s hip hop and I was a 90s junky.

"I am going to network my ass off in here. Let's go walk over there though, towards the food," Nicole pointed. We nodded our head in agreement.

I walked past a few former clients I had written for and then the editor of Jade Magazine walked over to Claire and I. "Ladies!" She held up her drink in an attempt for an in impromptu toast.

"Merlyn," I leaned in and hugged her and so did Claire. "Great gathering here. I am excited about the new launch of the magazine."

She eyed Claire and I and smirked, "Excited enough to join on as freelancers?"

"Freelancers?" Claire and I said in unison. I added, "You want us to contribute to what?"

"Your own column, "From the Pen of Claire and Janet", I have always loved that about you two."

I looked at Claire, she wasn't frowning and that's when I knew that she was interested. I turned to Merlyn. "It sounds like quite an idea. Let's meet about it this week. If we can work my sister in who is a freelance photographer I think we can do it."

Merlyn eyed me and laughed, "Always loved your spunk. Here take my card, call the office. Let's set it up this week. Okay ladies off to mingle. Ciao."

"Slick to throw Nicole in there," Claire said, walking in the direction Nicole had taken.

"I have to always look out for my girls, you know that."

"I agree. Now let's eat before someone else stops us."

We had become nose deep into the appetizers they had laid out for the crowd. I had already eaten three of those cheesecake bites and I was eyeing a fourth when Claire nudged me. "Please don't let the hood come out of you but your boy just stepped into this party."

I turned following the direction of her eyes and gasped. My heart sunk and my eyes grew furious. But as quickly as I became angry, I changed it to being nonchalant. "Oh I see."

Nicole nudged me and asked, "That's your man? Denim?"

"He's not my man. He's a friend."

Claire eyed me and I couldn't tell if she was confused or disgusted. "What the hell you mean he ain't your man?"

"We agreed that we wouldn't have any attachments. No titles, no strings, no commitment," I blurted trying to find my next drink from an unsuspecting server walking around.

"Did his trifling ass force you to agree to that stupid ass rule?" Claire was angry. I could see the veins in her neck pulsating. I shushed her and told her to calm down.

"No, he didn't. I halfway was the initiator. We agreed together actually."

"You?" Claire and Nicole said in unison.

"Yeah me!"

"Why on earth would you tell that man you don't want any attachments? I've seen the way you two look at each other. Hell, I've seen how your ass walks around all damn day smiling for no reason. Why wouldn't you want more?" Claire didn't give me a chance to respond as she went on and on.

"Love is very difficult. I am trying to limit some of the same mistakes I made in the past and laying low on titles seems like the right thing to do."

"Girl please. Love is easy. It's people who are difficult. Hence this stupid ass rule you two created. It ain't gonna work," Nicole blurted.

"Watch!"

I walked away in search of Denim. I could hear Nicole and Claire as they tried to follow close behind me. I turned and eyed them warning them to not be so obvious.

There he was seated at a table with Ms. Tight Skirt. She was cute, but I definitely didn't want to seem jealous. Oh but I was. This negro said he was going to be in the studio not on a date. His friend Dalvin was with him and had some cute young thing on his arm as well. Oh so this is how they do? Both hoe ass negros.

I tried to change the thoughts in my head from sounding like a woman scorned but hell, who was I fooling? If Denim was going to go out it needed to be with me on his arm. Not Ms. Tight Skirt. Then I thought why? That man owes you nothing. Or does he?

I got tired of listening to the stupid chick in my head and turned on my heels not knowing that his friend Dalvin saw me and had put Denim on notice. I looked at Claire and Nicole and said, "Let's go back to our section."

Nicole's eyes looked big and she turned around swiftly. "Your boy just spotted you walking away. He looks busted. Not the look of an unattached man if you ask me."

"Walk ladies, back to our section."

Knowing that he was looking made me nervous. He knew that I saw him so I turned around and gave him a blank face. No expression. Just blank. Then I turned back around to find seats of our own. Why I did that I don't know. But I knew I would have to explain it later.

Denim

"I'd stand in the shadows of your heart and tell you that I'm not afraid of your dark."- Andrea Gibson

That quote was emailed to me earlier today from a client and I didn't understand it. Hell I kind of still don't. I wasn't the romantic kind; I was the wooing kind when I wanted to just show off. But no woman got anything special from me. What was considered special when it came to me anyway?

Janet was a woman designed specifically for a purpose in my life. What that specific purpose was I was still trying to figure out. How can a person I have never known make so much sense to me? It was as if I had known her for years. She understood me; she never questioned why I was so passionate about music and beats because just like me she was in love with art too. Just art of a different kind. She was in love with words. She made melodies with her fingers every day when she wrote. So I understood her passion. I understood her love for it and when she understood mine I grew closer to her.

I was supposed to be in the studio tonight but the session got cancelled. Don't ask me why didn't I ask Janet to come to me to this event, I don't know. But Lena was there. So I asked Lena. To be honest I had been spending so much time with Janet that I needed to limit my time with her. I had already told her that I loved her but shit, I was a man. I still wanted to act on my needs and so tonight I planned to.

Lena was my date but I had a session scheduled with Jessica later on. I had met her at the gym she was a trainer. Perfect body, great smile, and her conversations intrigued me. She was the perfect type of woman for me to release my desires on. I was anticipating that rush tonight.

I had made love to Janet unprotected. I had connected to her inner loins and I could still feel her around me. I could feel her breath on my skin, her hands rubbing up and down my back, her moans and cries still echoed within my mind. I hadn't made love to any woman in so many years that I knew that it was love when I met her. I knew it was love when I kissed her. I knew it was love with I was inside of her. I don't know why I loved her, I just did.

Sometimes you meet someone who just does it for you. I always heard about it. I've always wondered how old couples who had been married for years and years knew. I didn't get it until I had it for myself.

Soulmates do exist!

I wasn't even present at this event because all I was doing was thinking about her. I pulled my cell phone out to text her when Dalvin said, "Fire is about to be lit on your ass dog." I eyed him confused. "Your girl Janet just saw you. I think she was headed over here then she turned around."

"Janet?" Lena asked hearing her name. I shushed her and turned around. I saw her walking away and then she turned and looked directly at me.

"Shit!" I cursed under my breath.

Once she witnessed my reaction, Lena began her mission to nag the hell out of me. "Oh so is she your woman now?" I held my finger up to her signaling for her to be quiet.

"What kind of look was that? It was like a challenge if you ask me?" Dalvin asked.

Hell, I didn't know either. I couldn't tell you what the hell that woman was thinking right now.

"She's upset!" I replied.

"Well, fuck yeah she's upset bro. Didn't you tell her that you were going to be at the studio? Damn and that look though." Dalvin was laughing. I didn't see anything funny.

"Dude shut up!" I shot back. I looked over to Lena. "I don't want to hear it. You know where we stand." She closed her mouth and became tightlipped and then rolled her eyes and turned her back to me. I waved her off and then turned back around to see if I could still see Janet. I couldn't.

I rose up out of my seat and went in search for her. "I'll be right back."

"I'm so sure!" Lena called out before I could step away. I chose not to respond. Now was not the time anyway.

I walk across the room. I think she was wearing a red dress. For the life of me I couldn't remember what she was wearing. The only thing I can remember was the look on her face. I couldn't read her and that pissed me off.

There she was. Seated with her friend and someone else. I figured she was her sister because they shared a lot of the same features. I walked over to her, placing my hands in my pocket and preparing for whatever reaction I was going to get. With her back to me her friends saw me first. Their expressions read here we go let the drama begin.

"Hey!" I said to her back. "Hi ladies," I said to her friends. Janet turned around slowly and nodded her head.

"Hey."

"Can I talk to you for a minute?" When she didn't reply I looked at her friends hoping they would help a brotha out and they did.

"Hi Denim, I'm Claire. We've seen each other before but never officially met."

I extended my hand and shook hers.

"Hi Claire nice to meet you. I turned to the other lady. And nice to meet you."

She took my hand. "Nicole, I'm Janet's baby sister."

"Yes, yes, yes, okay I figured you were related because you two look so much alike."

"That we do. So…well Claire and I are going to the dessert bar. Feel free to have a seat because if we don't leave Janet won't talk to you." Nicole and Claire got up and walked away. I took their advice and sat down next to Janet.

"She's just a friend," I quickly said.

"I'm not tripping D, you're a grown man. Do as you wish," Janet shot back. She was tough.

"I know I'm grown Janet. I was going to be in the studio tonight but the session got cancelled."

"And your phone broke too. Dang it must have been a bad day." She arrogantly took a sip of her drink and then eyed me as if she was challenging me to say something.

"No, I just didn't think to call. Look, we've been spending a lot of time together. I wasn't trying to crowd you. That's not what we are about. It's supposed to be free, easy you know."

She didn't immediately reply and when she did her face was softer. "Yep you're right. Easy and free. I am not tripping. You don't owe me an explanation."

"I know that babe. I just feel like I should explain myself. Lena was there so I just decided to bring her to this event. It was last minute anyway."

She nodded her head nonchalantly. "Okay! I'm going to go ahead and leave. I'm pretty familiar with this crowd anyway. Enjoy your night."

Janet rose up so quickly that I didn't get a chance to respond before she grabbed her purse and began to walk away. I grew angrier by the second. I didn't do anything wrong. What was the big deal anyway? She knew what was up.

Janet

I placed my phone down on the dresser and ran into my bathroom to freshen up. I only had five minutes. I loved when he surprised me like this. I decided to wear my favorite pink boy shorts with the matching polka dot cotton shirt that hung off my left shoulder. I sprayed on some of my favorite Carol's Daughter oil mist and massaged it into my skin.

I popped on some gloss and then went into the living room and dimmed my lights. It was exactly five minutes later when I heard the ringing of my doorbell. I giggled to myself and rubbed my hands together. Placing my hand on the doorknob, I took a deep breath and opened the door. "Hey you!"

"Hey baby." Paul stepped in looking as sexy as he wanted to be. I couldn't wait to sit in his lap. I laughed to myself.

"You look nice. Come on in. I just finished cooking if you want something to eat." I knew how saying that would lead him straight to my bedroom. Let's see if I was going to be right.

"Yeah baby I am hungry." Paul snatched me by the waist and pulled me into him. I smiled widely. "I came just for you."

"For me?" I purred.

"For you!" He lifted me in his arms in one swift move and walked me into my bedroom. He laid me down in the middle of my bed and said, "You look wonderful babe."

I whispered, "Thank you."

I watched him step out of his shoes, unbuckle his pants, and drop them. He lifted his shirt over his head and my eyes danced around as they become familiar again with the curves of his chest, the ripeness of his abs, that that sexy V that led down to his warrior. I purred anticipating when I was going to see his tool.

He climbed over to me and told me to sit up. I do. He pulled my cotton shirt over my head and reached for my hair. He slowly pulls the scrunchy that held my hair together down causing my hair to fall across my shoulder ticking the base of my back. "I love you with your hair down." He says just before kissing me.

I lay back as he trails his hands over my hair, down my face, across my neck bone, down my breast, and he massages my belly. I moan and shivered because his touch was so soft, so passionate, so perfect. "I like that," I whispered.

"I love how your skin feels." He complimented me again. This man is on one tonight, huh?

I shivered and my hips jerked when he graced his hand across my kitty forcing me to widen my legs. He reached to my waistline and pulled down my shorts and my panties at the same time and in no time I was naked as the day I was born. My breast fell to the side as my belly rose up and down breathing deep and heavy to grasp the desire I had burning inside of me.

Paul once again forced me to open my legs. I felt as if I was getting my annual checkup my legs were so wide. I was grateful that I had trimmed my kitty. She was bare, smooth, and ready to go. I could smell the sweet scent of my nectar escape into the night's air. It danced over the bed and its scent was so strong Paul raised up above me and inhaled deeply.

He blew out air and said, "Baby you smell so damn good. Is she wet for me?" Wet? That kitty is leaking so bad my mattress will be a waterbed soon.

I purred in the sexiest voice I could create under such pressure, "She is Daddy. She is so wet for you. Taste her. I want you to drown in her juices. I want you to see just how happy she is to see you." I made sure my voice was pleading. I wanted this man to know I wanted him in the worst way. Besides Head Hunter always had to live up to his name.

He buried his face inside of me dipping his tongue in my puddle of passion. I arched my back and pushed my hips further into his face. I couldn't even hold the first orgasm. I squirted all over of his face and when I heard him slurping my juices I began to shake as if electricity was being shot though my body. uncomfortably . The convulsions were evidence of a back to back orgasm. I screamed out "I'm coming" so loudly the orgasm made me lose control of my limbs.

Paul hooked his arms around my thighs forcing me to be stuck in one position. I squirmed and screamed, and he didn't let up. He buried his faced deeper within my kitty, licking and sucking and dipping. I nearly passed out because the next explosion was so powerful. I gripped my bedding so hard the mattress began to turn inward.

My eyes rolled to the back of my head as I laughed out and shook my head. "Oh my goodness!" I called out.

Paul moaned, released my legs, and hopped off the bed placing on our protection in a matter of seconds. Returning to me, he positioned himself on top and dipped his head in my hole. He pulled it out just to dip it halfway in again. I cried out for him to stop teasing me but he didn't. And pow orgasm number three was making its debut. I cried out I was coming and just when I felt the mass explosion reach its peek Paul pushed himself inside of me and my entire being grasped him.

I could hardly breathe as Paul was pounding deep within my loins. He kissed me so deeply. He squeezed me so passionately. He made me feel like I had the best kitty ever created. I held onto the man climbing on top and giving him the ride of his life. After all, he deserved it. I rode that warrior seeing if I could match his talents.

€€€I turned over on my left side and stretched. I glanced at my clock and saw that it read 1:30 am. Turning to my right I rubbed my eyes to get a clear picture and noticed Paul stretched out, ass naked. We must have fallen asleep.

I reach for my cell and noticed I had several missed calls. I noticed a few texts and scrolled through them. A few were from Denim, asking to talk. That was sent at eleven p.m. I rolled my eyes and placed my phone back down. I need this man to roll his ass on up out of here. No wonder I woke up. It was almost always impossible to sleep with someone else in my bed.

I sat up on the side of my bed and allowed my feet to hang off the railing. I scooted off and made my way into my bathroom. After emptying my bladder I walk into the kitchen naked as the day I was born to get a glass of water.

The cold liquid cooled me. Turning on my heels, I screamed in fear. "Boy you scared me."

Paul walks over to me and kisses my forehead. "I heard you walking around. Can I get a bottle of water?" I reached back into the fridge to fetch him one.

Handing him the bottle I asked, "On your way out right?"

After taking a huge swallow he breathes out, catching his breath. "Damn woman you're gonna make me leave in the middle of the night?"

"You know the rules Paul." I walked past him into my room and began to search for my clothes.

He follows in behind me, "We've been fucking for what a year? You mean to tell me you don't feel anything for me?" I know this man did not just ask me this.

I stared at him blankly switching my weight to one hip and said, "Um what? Paul really are we going there tonight?"

He waved me off and said, "You know what nah we ain't going nowhere."

He marches over to his clothes and starts to put them on with just a little more attitude than necessary if you ask me. I rolled my eyes and decided to play nice. I sat on the chair next to my bed and said, "Paul are you okay? You asked that question for a reason. So talk to me."

"I'm cool Janet. I know what it is."

I placed my hand on his shoulder. "You want to meet up this week for lunch or something. My treat?"

For a minute I thought he was going to turn me down but I had to keep him in my good graces. I needed him to please me on demand and if he left angry I knew I would have to work at getting him back on my good side. "Yeah, that's fine." I kissed his forehead when I heard a knock.

I looked around as if someone had invaded my room and whispered, "Who the hell is knocking on my door." I crept over to the window and saw a black Range Rover. Oh my God!

I looked at Paul who stared at me and smacked his lips. "What?"

"Can you go out the back door?"

"The back door? What the hell, Janet are you serious?"

I walked over to him and got on my knees before him. "Please I will make it up to you. I just can't let this guy see you here."

"So you're seeing someone?" OMG if he just don't leave out the back door. Why the one hundred and one questions.

"No, I am not but I just don't want him to know. I will call you tomorrow. I promise." I snatched his jacket off the chair and stomped to the back of my house. He didn't say anything either and I'm sure he was pissed. Hell I was pissed because Denim decided to do a midnight drop by at my house and may have messed things over with Head Hunter. He better have a good reason to be at my door.

Once Paul was out , I rushed to the front of the house to get Denim inside as soon as possible just in case Paul wanted to act special and tell on me. I was glad Paul just parked across the street making it seem like one of my neighbors perhaps had a visitor. I couldn't come off as a hypocrite to Denim, not tonight. My nerves couldn't take it.

I swung open my door and said, "Um it's damn near two am!"

"You weren't answering your phone. Had to make sure you were alright," Denim said walking into my living room. "Nice place too."

I closed the door making sure to peek out to see if Paul came walking around. He didn't. "Thanks and um because I don't answer doesn't mean I'm not okay or that you can just pop up."

"Yes it does." He took a seat on my couch.

"And why is that?"

"Because when I call or text you always reply."

"Sounds cocky."

He shot back, "Sounds true."

"So I'm good. I'm alive you see. What else do you want?"

"Nothing. Come sit next to me." I immediately became nervous. My bed was disheveled and I had Paul all in my pores. What was I going to do? Oh yeah act mad.

"Nah definitely don't want to crowd your space tonight. I'll sit over here." I sat in my love seat making sure he couldn't sit next to me.

Denim laughed and said, "You left the event kind of angry tonight."

I pointed to my chest and sarcastically asked, "Did I? Oh no, I was good. We're good?"

"Really you're going to act like that? You know I know you."

I rolled my eyes. "Oh so now you know me?"

"Of course. The connection we have is way beyond our control. I feel you, I can hear you when I am not with you, and I can sense you are getting wet right now. I can feel your heartbeat from here Janet."

I rolled my eyes and eyed him. "You're wrong." I wanted to scream inside because he was so right. Hell I had just experienced six orgasms with Mr. Head Hunter himself I didn't need anymore. But it was Denim. It was him. I couldn't go there. Not dirtied up like I was.

Denim laughed and said, "Okay have it your way Janet. I'm wrong, you're right."

I waved him off. "Whatever. So um I'm going to go to bed. It's late." I needed him to leave before he smelled Paul on me.

"Cool I'm sleepy too."

"You want to spend the night?" Oh my God, I am being punked right now.

"Yeah, why not?"

THE *[illustration]* I Didn't Say

I had to be a little upfront here and to be myself some time. "Okay I didn't expect company so let me go tidy up my room. I don't want you to see how I really am. And I am not asking. I am telling you. Just wait."

Denim raised up his hands. "Fine okay!"

I marched into my room and locked the door. I frantically looked out the window to see if Paul's car was gone from across the street. I ran to my bathroom's linen closet and grabbed some new sheets. I felt I was running a marathon.

Once the bed was made, I found a Summer's Eve douche, squirt the liquids up my kitty, and did a quick wash off with some water and soap. I wiped my neck, belly, in between my legs and my thighs. I lastly did one spray of my Prada perfume and then marched out into my room.

I unlocked my bedroom door and called out, "You can come in." My mouth dropped when I saw Paul seated across from Denim. What the hell?

Denim

I had my nose turned up at Janet. It was only a few hours ago she was acting like the victim. Hurt and crushed to see someone else on my arm. But no, here she was actually at her home with someone else. "She had you leave out the back door?" I asked him.

Now I could care less what the man said. But I was going to milk this shit. I was going to make Janet feel lower than the shit underneath my shoe. But the dude was whack. I wasn't going to answer the knock on the door but I figured I would help Janet out while she tried to clean up whatever she was hiding. To my surprise, Homie the Clown was standing in her doorway and asked, "So are you her nigga?"

I frowned. What man does that? Hell if I was Janet I would tell you to go out the back door too pulling some weak ass move like this. I shook my head and tried not to laugh. I guess this was his effort to make me leave. So he could win I guess. I wanted to say Dude; you have just made my job way easier. She will never want you after this.

But no, I kept quiet pretending that I was somewhat upset with this awkward situation. And it was definitely awkward. It was so uncomfortable that I had to readjust myself in my pants and create some more room for my balls to breathe. Shit was getting hot in here.

Janet's expression was priceless. Yeah sending him out the back door didn't work. I wanted to laugh so badly. I wanted to tell her that her so called pimping skills sucked. That she could learn a thing or two from me. Then I thought, well I did just pop up over her house.

"What the hell?" Janet asked walking out into the living room. "Didn't I have you leave?"

I raised an eyebrow and half way felt bad for the guy. That's the first thing you say? She had no sympathy for the guy and then that's when I understood his level in her life. He had none.

"This is fucked up Janet. You are wrong in this situation," he blurted back.

"Paul how am I wrong? You aren't my man. So what is this; you came back to tell on me?" She then turned and threw her hand my way. "He ain't my man either. So who's mad?"

Damn she was cutthroat. I was kind of turned on by this. Perhaps I should have felt embarrassed that I was turned on but nope I wasn't. I had never seen a woman like Janet. To react the way that she did in a situation such as this was rare and almost unheard of. She had the type of control I possessed.

He looked at me and then back at her. "Look Janet enough is enough. Let me be upfront with you."

Janet folded her arms across her chest. "Please do because I ain't ever lied to you, gave you false hope or empty promises. So what's up because you really just did a number on me with this one?"

"And making me leave out the back door was cool with you?"

"I mean I'm sorry. I just didn't want to be doing what it is we are doing right now, standing in an awkward ass situation—"

I interrupted and said, "So I know I maybe shouldn't say anything but, Paul, that's your name right, go ahead and speak your mind. I definitely want to hear this." Janet eyed me with a stare that read shut the hell up. I winked at her.

Paul threw up his hands in surrender. "It doesn't fucking matter. Janet I got you. Enjoy your fucking night." He stormed across the living room and slammed the door on his way out.

Janet looked at me and shrugged, "Damn I feel bad." Her tone was sarcastic.

"As you should. The back door though? You made the man leave out the back?" I couldn't hold my laughter but Janet grew angrier once she realized I was laughing at her.

"Look I only made him leave out the back because I didn't want to hear your mouth after what happened earlier."

"You mean you didn't want to come off as a hypocrite?" Janet didn't respond. I walked over to her trying to compose my laughter. "It's cool baby girl. I'm not tripping. See this is how you should have reacted towards me earlier." I kissed her forehead giving her a bear hug in the process.

"Whatever!"

I slapped her on her ass and said, "Now off to bed. But definitely take a shower first. I am not trying to be rubbing all up on Paul. If you know what I mean." I arrogantly walked into her bedroom and made myself comfortable ignoring the dangerous stare she gave me for calling her out as she walked into her bathroom.

A couple months later…

Janet

"When love is not madness it is not love."- Pedro Calderón de la Barca

It was weird feeling safe in his arms at this very moment. I wanted to tell him to lie on his side of the bed but each time I muster up the strength to do so he would somehow pull me into him tighter. His hands felt perfect. I know many have said that statement before. But this one I really meant. I felt his fingers were creating memory trails across my flesh becoming familiar with my curves.

I shivered at the constant trailing of his hand down my bare back to the mount of my ass. He whispered he loved how my waist led to a round booty. "Fat!" He playfully whispered giving it a light slap. I smiled brightly, pushing myself further into him. I secretly was happy I was lying in a dark room with him. I wouldn't dare want him to see the smile he put on my face.

I buried my face into his neck and took a deep breath. I loved the way he smelled. It wasn't strong it was mild, sweet, and sort of boyish. He had a signature scent. If I didn't smell him again for ten years once reacquainted with it I would instantly know. I would know Denim.

His bare chest was so strong. Not a bit of fat on his belly. You would think his hard shell would be uncomfortable to lie on but it wasn't. It felt as if I had been here before. I hadn't known this man but for a few months and I felt as if he was a missing part of me. Our breathing matched, our sense of humor matched, he knew how to make me smile, he knew when I was mad, and he knew how to push my buttons.

Imagine a world without this feeling. Imagine a world where no one ever completed you. That the only thing that would connect you two was the fact you were just physically attracted to one another. That wasn't this. This wasn't that. This was something more.

Wrapping my arms around his waist, I give him a tight squeeze rubbing my nose back and forth across his neck. He never minded my doing that. He didn't mind me inhaling his flesh, inhaling his aura, inhaling the very breath he breathed. He actually welcomed it.

"I never let anyone in this close," he whispered.

I couldn't lie that the night's darkness added a sense of security to our wounded hearts. It was easier to be vulnerable if we couldn't actually see each other. The feeling was more ironically powerful. To feel him was way more impressionable upon my heart than his words because when I felt him I knew he was real. I knew this was real.

"Me either," I replied. I closed my eyes and squeezed them really tight. I was becoming emotional but I wasn't sad. Every time I held him close to me forever was all that I could ever see. I wanted to freeze these moments in time. I could live a lifetime in moments such as these.

"I hate to see you go," I cried out. I laughed in my head because he wasn't going anywhere but downtown to his studio. But seconds felt like minutes, minutes felt like hours, hours felt like days, days felt like weeks. If I went a day without seeing him I felt a disconnect. That disconnection felt as if my life was incomplete. He was completing my very being and that scared me.

I had no choice but to love this man. From that very first moment we met in the restaurant all those weeks ago, I knew. I had known then that I had loved him.

"I know babe. I know. You should come down today."

"Come down?"

That seemed like a couple's thing. It didn't matter how much we said I love you. It didn't matter how much we wanted to be together because we both always kept it free. No strings. No attachments. Funny thing is the only unattached thing we were doing was saying that we didn't want any attachments. We were falling in love with each other every day. We fell in love each time we kissed, each time we touched, each time we spoke.

"Yeah, think about it."

I grew quiet.

"Let's not say goodnight until the very last minute okay?"

He nodded his head. I could feel him in the dark. "Okay babe. Okay."

€€€

I walked into Kelvin's office and smiled brightly. I hadn't seen him in a couple weeks. We had kind of fallen out after the night I first kissed Denim. I mean I had fallen out with all of my old guys so I had to go out and get some new ones. Just for a distraction. I felt the more guys I had on the back up list the safer I would be from the wrath of Denim's love.

Seeing men like Kelvin kept me balanced weirdly enough. I felt that having sex with them would keep me from falling so hard for a man I've waited all my life for. Sounds stupid but call it what you want. I didn't want to get hurt. I didn't want to give that man my all, not yet that is. And so I visited my others. I had sex with them, I dined with them, and it was all for a distraction from the obvious.

"Hey you, how have you been?" Kelvin greeted me and led me into his office. "What are you doing over this way?"

"I came downtown to see some folks about a project and I wanted to stop by and say hey to you." I kissed his cheek before taking a seat.

He looked at me up and down and licked his lips. "Hmm you look nice today babe."

I seductively crossed my legs. "Do I now?"

"That you do." He came from across his desk and took a seat on the edge of his desk in front of me. "You look really good," he said again.

I smiled widely and licked my lips too. My clit began to perform jumping jacks in my lace thong as my eyes began to study Kelvin's statuette . Leaning back in the chair I cross and uncross my legs then I opened them widely just for Kelvin to get a good view.

He looked at my kitty. "Damn baby." His voice was low and groggy as I eyed the bulge in his pants.

"Yes?" I asked nearly dominating his line of sight.

He stood up then slowly lowered himself to his knees. I held up my hands. "Wait go and lock the door." While he ran to do as I asked I lifted up my ass and slipped out of my thong, tossing it at my feet so that he could see. Then I spread my legs so wide my lips opened revealing my pearl tongue. "Taste her," I purred.

Kelvin returned to me dropping to his knees. He leaned in and kissed my lips. "Scoot closer to me," he whispered.

I giggled following his command. "Yes sir!"

I could smell my essence escape into the air as I felt my juices ooze through my lips. Its sweet smell of cherry and vanilla oils, I used this morning planting some in between my thighs, was mixed with my scent. I scooted further down so that I wouldn't get my cream on his office chair. I allowed my head to fall backwards and as I closed my eyes I took a deep breath to wait for impact.

I shivered at the initial contact from his warm wet tongue. He kissed me softly there with his lips. I knew my pearl tongue was breaking through the crevices of my lips when I felt his tongue pluck it. I moaned out in approval grabbing the back of his head and pushing him further into my kitty.

He greedily rubbed his lips and nose over my wetness as my desire for my orgasm to escape rushed to the surface.

Drip.

Drip.

Drip.

I knew it was a puddle of my cream drizzling its way out of my kitty, down Kelvin's chin and onto the floor. I covered my mouth as the strong impact of my orgasm became unbearable. Kelvin moaned in between pecks as I felt him rummaging with his pants. When I heard his zipper pull down I tilt my head to witness his self-pleasuring. Damn his dick is beautiful.

He grabbed himself with so much force I had to clinch my walls wishing that the impact of his dick was in my kitty and not his hand. Kelvin growled loudly slipping from his position leaning upward as I recognized his face upon climaxing. I watched his reaction to our sex. That always turned me on.

With his seed oozing from his tip and over his hand I slowly push upward, closing my legs together to catch my falling juices. I eyed his box of tissues and did a quick wipe. Rising up I kiss Kelvin on his forehead and promise to see him later. I didn't even wait for him to stand up before I unlocked his office door and walked out. Besides the main reason I was downtown was to see Denim, Kelvin was just an added bonus.

Denim

I think every guy should have a Becky in his life. A Becky is a white woman, willing and able to do just about anything sexually that you desire. I rubbed my dick in circular motions as my very own personal Becky waltzed over towards me. Okay it may sound disrespectful to say but this Becky here was actually named Becky and this Becky here also just so happened to do whatever it is that I asked of her. Without the protesting and telling me what she isn't going to do. See that's the perfect combination for any man who just needs a release.

She would suck my dick for an hour if that's how long it would take me to cum. She would let me go in her ass, and she was willing and able to do whatever whenever. I rubbed my hands together from watching her slowly walk over towards me. I was hard just because of the anticipation of what was about to happen. I moaned quietly. My Becky.

I had given my artist a thirty minute break, Lena was off to get us some food, and my engineer was on the rooftop. The studio door was locked and it was just Becky and I.

"How have you been?" She asked me as I turned around in my chair to face her.

"Busy!" I responded. My voice just above a whisper. My tone robotic and my demeanor slouched.

"It's good to see you." She purred and kneeled down before me. I felt my dick jump in my pants. This girl wasted no time. She was on her knees and eyeing my package. "It's good to see him too." Reaching for my zipper she pulled it down and placed her hands inside my pants; she pulled him out.

THE ████ I Didn't Say

My head fell backwards at the initial touch of her hands on my dick. I could hear her licking her lips and smacking them as if she saw something appetizing. My body completely fell into a trance; eyes shut, arms to my sides, and I allowed Becky to go to work.

I felt the motions of her mouth. It was warm, wet, strong, and then soft. She moved in motions I knew only a Becky would know. Grabbing the back of her head, I allowed my hands to get lost in her blonde strands while pushing her mouth further into my lap. I could feel the tightening of the walls of her throat smother my head. I winced in approval forcing her to take me deeper inside of her mouth.

I allowed my mind to escape into what I was feeling. I allowed myself to enjoy this. I needed this. I wanted this. Here I was getting the pleasure that my dick badly needed and Janet's face appears. My eyes pop open as I try to understand why now. Why now of all times? I had been successful in the past with pushing her out when I was with other women, but right now at this moment, I was pretending that Becky was her.

Wait maybe if I imagine that Becky is Janet I would get the best of both worlds. I could get the amount of pleasure Becky gives with the one that I actually wanted, Janet. Janet would always be my center of pleasure. I moaned and became impatient. I felt my ass push itself inward as my dick became a brick. It was hard, so hard I growled. I grab Becky's head and nearly jammed myself into the back of her throat. I could hear her wincing and moaning but it wasn't pleasurable moans. It was moans of agony. But I couldn't stop. I held her head captive in my hands.

I could feel Becky trying to push off. Pushing on my waist, she uses all the force she could manage to muster up and cried out. I fell forward feeling myself about to explode. I growled, losing control of Becky's head. She fell backwards as my seeds fell all over the floor. Grabbing her mouth Becky cried out, "What the fuck was that Denim? I said stop!"

I looked at her suddenly remembering who it was before me. Her eyes were glossy and filled with fear and confusion. She was afraid of me? Wait what happened?

"What?" I asked catching myself and leaning on the soundboard. I began to pull my pants up and attempted to zip them. "What are you talking about?"

Becky cried out, "You were hurting me. And who the hell is Janet?"

I eyed her with confusion. "Wait, what did you say?" What the hell was wrong with me? Did I really just call this woman Janet? When had I ever made such an amateur mistake such as this? "I'm sorry. I got caught up."

Becky stood to her feet and wiped her mouth with the back of her hand and then her eyes. She was crying. I walked over toward her but she threw her hands up and told me not to come near her. Damn I had messed up.

"I'm sorry."

"Whatever Denim." Rolling her eyes, she turned on her heels grabbing her bag and rushing towards the door. She pulls it open and Janet appears in the doorway.

"Janet!" I yelled out.

Becky turned to me and her look was devious. As if she felt like she struck gold. "So you're Janet?" She eyed me and smirked turning her attention back to Janet. I rushed over towards her and placed my hand on the door so that Janet could walk in and Becky could walk out.

"Hey babe come on in. Becky thanks for today. I'll talk to you later." I pushed Becky on her lower back towards the door. Janet stared at the both of us and gave Becky a weak hello.

"Hi," Janet said, waltzing in and lastly taking her stance to the middle of my studio. Becky smacked her lips and rolled her eyes. I pushed her outward telling her goodbye one more time.

"Hmm that was interesting," Janet said, folding her arms across her chest.

THE ![image] I Didn't Say

I gave her a weak smile and said, "You're early babe." I gave her a rough kiss on her cheek rubbing my hands over my jeans.

Janet laughed and rolled her eyes. "Really, a white woman? I am in the twilight zone. You're fucking a white woman and she ain't even cute either."

"Huh? Wait, what babe?" I said, turning around and taking a seat in my chair.

Janet was laughing hard now. Slamming her hand down on the counter top she said, "Denim look at you. Your body language is a dead giveaway. Wait, were y'all in here sexing it up?" She took a look around and gave me a look of disgust.

"Babe I don't know what you are talking about," I stared at her blankly.

Janet rolled her eyes and blew out air. "I swear I am trying to understand why you told me to come down here at the same time you are fucking a white bitch. My mind doesn't quite understand this mess."

"Babe I didn't have sex with that woman."

"Look at me Denim. I am going to give you an out. I am going to give you the opportunity to look me in the eyes and not lie to me."

I threw my hands up and they landed loudly on my lap. "I didn't."

I stared at Janet straight in the eyes. I stared at her telling her that lie. I knew she knew I was lying but I was hoping that she would just let it go, that she would just leave it be and take my answer but I knew her. I knew Janet all too well and I knew that she wouldn't.

Janet dropped her head. Her chin hitting her chest and I could tell she was going over the words to say in her head. I swallowed hard and waited to see what she was going to say. I was hoping the interrogation had ended and she had accepted my answer.

She lifted her right hand and pointed at the floor. "You didn't fuck her, so why is your seeds all over the floor?"

My eyes widen as I looked in the direction in which she was pointing and my mouth hung low. My words caught in my throat. I didn't know what else to say. I wanted to say that it wasn't what she thought it was. But that shit wasn't going to work right now.

"I…I…babe listen." She threw up her hand and laughed.

"I'm good Denim. I'm so good. I'll holla at you later." She didn't look back as she walked away. And when she was out of the room I just stared at the wet spot on the floor and shook my head.

Yeah, I guess everyone doesn't really need a Becky after all.

Janet

I walked into my office throwing my briefcase on my desk. I had been getting nonstop calls and texts from Denim. But was I going to answer them? No. I plopped down in my chair lost in my thoughts. In my mind, I saw him with her and her with him and I cringed. Yuck!

"Chick I know you hear me!" Claire waltzed into my office forcing me to give her attention. I looked up and focused in on her. Hmm she seemed different. Her demeanor was different. She had a new aura around her. If I guessed it right, something or someone good has happened in her life. Hmm.

"Yes what's up?"

"Uh oh what happened? I can see it all over your face."

"Nothing happened."

"Was it Kelvin? I know you can't put too much emphasis on that man. He is never consistent."

"Apparently neither is Denim."

Claire took a seat in front of my desk. "Denim, why him? You two should be easy breezy with all this no attachment crap."

I huffed and puffed and switched around in my seat. "Yeah you're right but...oh nothing."

"Nothing my ass, what happened?"

"I walked in on him with a white woman!" I barked.

Claire's eyes grew wider as she studied me. "So you're mad because she's white or because he was with someone else?"

I sucked my teeth and rolled my eyes. "Really are you asking me that?"

"And I am waiting on an answer. You aren't fooling anybody but yourself if you think we all believe this unattached mess. You two are in love and all that wackiness. Y'all be in each other's face damn near every day. Or you are on the phone cheesing and shit all damn day. I don't get it."

"Titles bring problems," I shot back while powering up my laptop. I was trying to derail my attention from Claire's interrogation.

"Girl please. Apparently no titles bring problems too. Look at you. You can't even answer the question. I swear Denim and you are getting on my last nerve." She rose up from her seat and laughed. "I bet you were just with somebody else too. Like come on Janet. Let's be real."

"I know you aren't talking. Since you're all caught up in your running buddy."

"Oh you're bringing up Lewis now? Big difference is he just a friend."

"Sure Claire."

Claire waved her hand off at me and walked out then yelled out, "Oh here comes your…whatever he is to you now!"

I looked up and saw Denim. "Dude did you really just come here?"

Denim held up his hand signaling that he wanted me to be quiet. He walked in and closed the door to my office. "Babe listen. I know that situation was awkward. I know it was babe, but I didn't do anything we both aren't expecting me to do."

I grew quiet. What was I supposed to say? Oh yeah the truth. I just want it to be you and I. Wait I want it to just be him and I? That was the first time I admitted that to myself. I stood there quietly stuck in my own words as he asked question after question. I don't even know if I was even paying attention to him. I was staring in his direction but I wasn't actually listening.

"I don't want to talk about it." I waved him off. I felt stupid. He was right. We had agreed no strings. No commitment. He was stuck in his ways. I was stuck in my ways. Hell, would creating titles complicate things if we both were willing to be with other people?

THE ▓▓ I Didn't Say

Shit I don't know. I dropped my head in my hand and said, "Look I don't want to talk about it okay. You're right. That's established, now can we move on to the next subject?"

Denim walked over to me and placed his hands on my lower back and attempted to bend down. I jumped up from my seat and held out my hands in protest. He eyed me and frowned. "What?"

"I know you didn't shower in the thirty minutes from when She was on you. She's still on you." I cringed halfway disgusted. I pushed him backwards as he dropped his hands to his sides.

"Babe." He looked defeated. He was out of excuses. I knew I was right. That woman's bodily fluids were on him and here he was in my face. Like really, I wasn't some side piece of his. I was his... Damn what was I?

"I just wanted to come check on you and I wasn't thinking." He placed his hands in his pockets and continued, "I'm sorry about today. I know I shouldn't be, but it was awkward and I am sorry for that."

I frowned at him when he hinted that he actually shouldn't even be apologizing to me right now. I shook my head and awkwardly laughed, "You're right. Nothing is wrong. Go on and enjoy the rest of your day." I waved him off. "We're good. I promise."

Claire

I rushed into my bathroom grabbing my bottle of Chanel Number Five perfume and gave it two splashes across my flesh. I gave myself a once over in the mirror and smiled at what I saw. The weeks of maintaining my commitment to run five miles every other day was now working its magic. My skin was radiating and my hair was thick and bouncy. My stomach was nearly flat as a board, my ass was sitting up, and my calves were strong and firm. I was hot. Hell I was Ms. Fine As Wine.

I hadn't planned on seeing Evan at all tonight. Apparently he had some meeting that was running over its time. He asked for me to place his plate in the oven. He'll get a real shocker when he notices I didn't even cook for his ass. I laughed while staring at myself in the mirror. I was changing and I knew that. But I was happy and I knew that too.

I walked out of my bathroom and into my bedroom plopping down to place on my heels. I grabbed my clutch and my phone and whisked down the stairwell. I looked around the house once more and it was a tad bittersweet. I used to love coming home and being in this space.

I cherished and bragged about the decorations I did for each room. It was my castle that my King had given me. But now I didn't feel like I was married to a King. I felt like now I had an overseer, a caretaker. I had someone who only shared the same physical address with me. But your home is not where your zip code is, it's where your heart is. Where was Evan's heart?

Hell, where was mine? I didn't even know the answer to that. I gave a weak smile and turned on my heels out the front door. I didn't want to think about the reality the walls of my home had witnessed. I just wanted to smile tonight. I was going to smile with Lewis.

€€€

I pulled into the parking area and allowed valet to take my keys. I clenched my pearls and took a deep breath to soften my nerves. Lewis invited me out to a mixer with some of the elite doctors in the greater Atlanta area. Imagine how smitten I was to discover Lewis was a doctor. A cardiologist at that. I purred to myself just thinking about how my heart would be placed in his possession.

I shook my head and tried to get those thoughts out of my head. I smiled at the hosts who greeted me upon walking in. "Hello, how are you this evening?"

"I'm great. Can you point me in the direction of Dr. Stewart's party?"

"Hmm let me see here." She looked at the electronic screen and made small motions with her fingers across its surface until she found what she was looking for. "Claire Young? He's expecting you. Let me take you to your party."

I followed her up a ladder of stairs that led to an outside balcony. I heard Lewis's laughter before I even saw him. I smiled brightly to myself as I anticipated the first sight of him. He was without a doubt a light in my life right now. There was nothing bad about our communication. He was just that good for me. At least for right now he was. I mean all guys start off this good and then eventually they become like the rest of them. I was hoping that it wouldn't go south anytime soon.

The host pointed in the direction she wanted me to walk. I thanked her and continued my journey over. "Hello!"

Lewis sat at a table with four other gentlemen. They were all much older than he was. He wore a grey vest over a plum colored shirt, matching tie, and black shoes. He was handsome and he stood up with enough confidence to fill up three grown men.

He was ooo wee delicious. I licked my lips and forced myself out of my trance.

"Hey you!" Lewis walked over towards me and hugged me while kissing me on my cheek.

"Fellas this lovely lady here is Claire Young. She is a successful author. Claire these old guys are cardiologists like me."

"Old?" The oldest of the three called out as we all fell out in laughter.

I shook each of their hands as they all complimented me on my appearance this evening. Taking me by the hand Lewis led me away from the pack and off to the railing that overlooked the highways of downtown Atlanta.

"You look beautiful tonight Claire."

I blushed and smiled. I don't know why I struggled with staring Lewis in the eyes but I did. He was a tad bit too good to be true. He was handsome, a charmer, a doctor, and the conversations we had were effortless . I was more comfortable around him than my own husband.

"You managed to get away tonight." He motioned for a server to bring us a drink and took two glasses, handing me one.

"Yes I did. It actually wasn't as hard as you would think." Lewis and I barely talked about Evan but he knew about my marriage. Hell, he met me with a ring on my finger.

"In any event, I am glad to have you here with me tonight." The he leaned in and kissed me softly on my cheek. His motions were so slow, sensual, smooth, and original. It was as if he had never kissed anyone that way before. At least that's how he made me feel.

"I am glad I came too. I needed to get out. I needed to come to see you." I stuttered speaking these words but they seemed to find their way out. My open honesty was my desperate attempt at letting him know that I wanted him in the worst way. I dropped my head in embarrassment and chastised myself mentally. I hadn't slept with any other man in years. Why start now? Hell why not now Claire? Get it together and man up.

"Are you okay Claire?" Lewis took his index finger to my chin and pushed upward forcing me to look back up to him.

Taking a huge swallow of my drink I shook my head yes. "Something about you makes me act like a school girl."

Lewis eyed me and laughed. "Really? I was thinking the same about me. I go back twenty years talking to you Claire. We are good together."

I laughed slightly and for what seemed like forever we stared at each other until I bashfully looked away. "So what do you doc's do at these parties?"

"Nothing but show face really."

"Hmm sounds like a bore," I joked.

"I would be bored if you weren't here," Lewis boldly shot back.

I eyed him and asked, "You like jazz? Dancing?"

"Yeah whenever I get the chance I like to get down woman."

I laughed out and said, "Let's get our cars. Then you can follow me. I got somewhere I want to take you."

He laughed and gave me the side eye. "Lead the way lady. I'll follow."

€€€

Kat's Café was in full swing tonight. The live band had everyone on the dance floor or lined up around the walls hugging somebody from behind grooving to the beat. I smiled and pulled the two pins out of my hair that I was using to hold up a few strands. I shook my head lightly and called over to music to Lewis, "Let's get a real drink."

"Lead the way," Lewis called out over the music.

I ordered an Amaretto Sour and Lewis ordered a Hennessey straight. I winced at him and laughed, "Must I carry you home tonight after that drink?"

He laughed and patted my shoulder, "I got this little lady. You just focus on the view in front of you."

"Oh now I'm a little girl. Whatever," I laughed while grabbing my drink after the bartender sat it down. I brought the glass to my lips while staring at Lewis intensely. I boldly reached over to him and began to run my fingers through his natural hair. He wore it low, sort of how Eric Benet wore his hair after he cut off his locs. "Did you use to have locs?"

He nodded his head yes. "I like this cut on you," I added.

He smiled, taking a swallow of his strong liquor. "I like your hair down and flowing like this." Lewis ran his fingers through the curls I had just released from its pins.

He cupped the back of my head and I immediately felt myself succumb to his touch. I leaned down feeling the base of the stool beneath me and I exhaled happy that something could catch me. I was weak behind his touch. Maybe I grew weak because his touch was new and unfamiliar and that excited me beyond measure.

I slowly allowed my eyes to reopen just to see how close Lewis actually was to me. My eyes popped open in shock when I discovered his hazel stare daring my dark like the night eyes to stare at them back.

I wanted to drop my head and become that shy girl again but Lewis gave the back of my head a slight tug pushing it upwards to stay in its position. "Look at me," he whispered.

Look at him, why is he doing this? This is just too much. I don't know why all of a sudden I felt as if I didn't have control over my own thoughts let alone my own body. He was just a guy. Okay no he wasn't just a guy he was becoming The Guy. The one I dreamed about, the one who fed me life, the one that gave me this feeling.

In this moment Evan popped in my head. Why now of all the times to invade my psyche? Why now when I had this fine specimen of a man standing in front of me asking me to be free with him? I could see the desires building up in Lewis's eyes. Yes, I was married. But what did being married to someone really mean once the connection is broken?

THE ![icon] I Didn't Say

Should I put a halt to my desires because on paper it says I am his wife? Or should I...

I took a deep breath and whispered, "Looking at you now is hard."

"Why?"

"Because...because this feeling on me is so heavy. I don't know how to handle it. I don't know how to handle this."

Lewis let go of my head and with his hands he grabbed the both of my hands and squeezed. "That's the problem. I see why you are a writer Claire. You want to control the story; you want to control the outcome. But babe you can't do that with me. You have to just allow things to be."

"But Lewis isn't this wrong?"

"Wrong?" He frowned. "I know when something is wrong Claire and this is not wrong. How I feel about you isn't wrong. This isn't wrong. It can't be."

Was it the alcohol or his hormones talking, or was he actually being genuine with me? After all; it was I that had something to lose, not him.

"This is new to me."

"What's new babe?"

"This feeling."

He smiled. He had innocence about him that I trusted. He seemed to just want to be in my space for no reason at all. And get this, we actually fit. The time with each other was effortless. I wondered why of all the times in my life when I was looking for the one I met Evan and married him. And now I sit across from Lewis. Maybe I am jumping the gun here.

"Kiss me," he asked.

I leaned into Lewis as he sat on the bar stool, his legs slightly parted I squeezed in between him and the stool. My hip pressed against his hip. My chest pressed against his chest. My arms wrapped around his shoulders. My eyes were staring directly into his eyes. Nose to nose and mouth to mouth I lean in slowly suck in the last bit of air between us.

A slight smile escaped as I gently placed my lips on his. With each second our lips pressed further and further into one another until we slightly parted our lips and allowed our flavors to mix into one. His kiss was just the right amount of pressure, the right amount of pecks, and the right amount of moisture.

Ever had a kiss so passionate that your soul seeped through your pores making its way into the other person's very being? As if in that very moment your body was no longer yours. You were one heart. You were one body. You were one breath. In that moment you became each other. I just had the kiss of my life.

Janet

I was enjoying the beat underneath my feet. I moved my hips to the rhythm allowing my sisters and friends to surround me in laughter and dance along. I was having the time of my life tonight.

I had decided to push out what had happened with Denim and I yesterday and just have fun tonight. Besides he was right, he didn't do anything wrong except that he didn't tell me what I wanted to hear. Which was; that he was sorry and that he only wanted to be with me. But nope, of course he didn't say that. Why? Because I helped set up a perfect world for him. He's having his cake and eating it too.

I looked over towards Tanya and Jessica who met up with Nicole, Diamond, and I at Club Krave for a night of drinks and dancing and called out, "Let's order some wings and a bottle for our section."

They gave me the go head as I walked off the dance floor and over to our section with Nicole. I had paid for a table for us at Krave so that we could have our own space. Out of a lot of places in Atlanta to go, I enjoyed this one the most. It had just enough lighting to not be fooled by the ugly guys, it was clean, there was enough room to dance, the appetizers were delicious, and the drinks were always strong.

"Order a bottle of Ciroc and cranberry sis," Nicole said, plopping down on the seat.

I waved over a waitress and placed my order handing her my credit card. "My feet are killing me," I whined, slipping one of my red bottoms off.

"I am glad I came out with y'all tonight. Lately I have just been working and researching all damn day and night," Nicole whined.

"How's that position going for you at Juicy Magazine?"

"I love it but I may start doing freelance work for Atlanta Nightlife blog as well."

I smiled brightly and gave my sister a high five.

"Go on then with your bad self."

Our server walked over and places a martini in front of me. I asked curiously, "Is this for me?"

"Oh yeah a guy at the bar left this note and ordered you this mango martini. He said it was your favorite."

I looked over her shoulder and tried to eye the bar. "Oh he's gone now though," she added.

"What guy, how did he look?" Nicole added.

"Yeah, I want to know because this was my favorite drink but I haven't drunk it in a while," I said.

The server said, "He was average height, beige, dark hair, hazel eyes. That's all I can remember. Sorry ladies," she said nonchalantly as she walked off. She walked off but stopped midstride and said, "oh he did leave this note." I took it in my hand and studied it.

You are still a beauty like you always were Jan.

"Well girl enjoy your free drink damn. At least someone is buying you something."

"Who the hell is this calling me Jan. How would they know this is my drink though? I haven't drunk this in a couple years. It has to be an old ex." I was turning every which way in my seat trying to find a familiar face but saw nothing.

"Girl, if the man wanted to be seen he would have come over. Drink up. Hell you are getting on my nerves." Nicole pushed back on the lounge chair and laughed. I didn't see anything funny though. She knew me. She knew that I was a control freak and that I always needed answers.

I stared at the drink on my table and began to run through names in my head but who was I fooling. Over the past few years I was a rolling stone. I was the bed crusher. I was the kryptonite. Half of the men I slept with were one timers and I couldn't remember their names let alone their faces.

When I traveled to events, appearances, meetings, and industry parties I always had a local smash buddy. Always! So why was I trying to figure out who the hell gave me this drink? If I was smart I wouldn't even drink it. It could be poisoned.

I pushed the drink back and sat back in my seat when I heard, "So you don't trust my drink I see."

I felt the hairs on the back of neck rise in an eerie reaction to their voice. His voice. I know that voice. I looked over to Nicole who was able to see the person behind me and her eyes said it all.

I knew him. Nicole knew him.

"What in the world. What the hell are you doing here?" Nicole blurted out.

Although I was afraid to turn around and see who it was I couldn't wait any longer. I switched around in my seat and my eyes landed on him. I jolted upward and with my mouth hung open I blankly stared at him and said, "Desmond!"

Desmond Howard

"There is love of course. And then there's life, its enemy."- Unknown

She looked the same as when I had last seen her. It was the day of the accident. I hadn't planned on not telling her about my marriage. But then again I guess God had a funny way of revealing the lies I told.

"Janet!"

She still was beautiful. She hadn't aged one bit. I was in love with this woman at one point. She had given me everything. She was my biggest cheerleader, my support system, my best friend, my greatest love, but she was also very independent, obsessive over her work, and simply put just too strong.

I know I know to say she is too strong sounds unappreciative. But what's too strong? I loved that quality about any woman but it sometimes made it hard for me to lead her. Sometimes I felt like the bitch in the relationship.

"Desmond, what the hell? Wait what are you doing here? Last I heard you were in Philadelphia."

"It got cold," I answered nonchalantly.

"Well go buy a coat." Janet turned back around and sat down. I maneuvered around and walked into their section.

"Nah bro do not make yourself comfortable over here," Nicole blurted out.

I glanced over to her and gave her a teasing grin. "Hey snot nose," I teased.

She waved me off. "I am not that scrawny kid anymore Desmond. I grew up. Something you should think about doing."

THE  I Didn't Say

"Okay, okay little foot, scoot over."

I took a seat next to Nicole who gave me much attitude. I must admit it was eerie seeing them. I knew that Diamond was somewhere close. We had all grew up together back in Fort Worth, Texas. Janet was my first love.

"You look beautiful." I complimented her as my eyes danced around her smooth chocolate flesh.

"You look aged. What's up? What do you want?"

"It's been years, how are you?"

"I'm alive Desmond."

I clasped my hands together and took a deep breath. I knew this meet and greet wasn't going to be easy but I was never given the chance to speak to her after the accident. After I buried my wife we have never had any type of conversation.

"We should talk. I am in town for a week. We have to talk Janet. It's been years."

"It's crazy that I see you in a club requesting this of me. So you just so happened to be at the same club as I at the same time?"

"Yes, I am with some clients."

"So you didn't seek me out Desmond. You stumbled across me."

"No fate led us in this same space." I stood up and pulled out a business card. "Look stop being stubborn. Take my card and call me tomorrow. We need to talk." She refused to take my card so I sat it down on the table just as I heard a familiar nag.

"What the hell? When what, wait a minute what is this motherfucker doing here?" I heard Diamond's country voice way before I saw her and cringed.

Out of all the sisters Diamond was the least civil. I turned in the direction of her voice and gave her my best fake smile. "Diamond!"

"Lame ass!" She shot back. I noticed two other women with her. "What coffin did you step out of?

"Not funny Diamond."

"Not welcome here Desmond." She plopped down next to Janet as they both stared me on. Neither one of them were letting up on their stares from hell. I took a deep breath and placed my hands in my pockets.

"Tomorrow Janet, please. Or I'll just have to come to you." I walked off without saying anything else. It was way past the time for us to speak on what happened between us.

Janet

The server came and sat down my order as the girls dove in pouring drink after drink and grabbing handfuls of wings. I stared at Desmond's card and rolled my eyes. I tried my hardest not to seem emotional but I was. Seeing him was surreal. Seeing him was a slap in the face.

Nicole walked over to me and sat so close our thighs were meshed together. "Sis talk to me."

Diamond purposely stared me down as well, waiting for me to say anything. "Well what you got to say Ms. Jamison? Spill it already."

"I don't know what to say. Give me a shot first." I grabbed the bottle of alcohol and downed a huge gulp of its strong contents. I wince at the burning in my throat and belched. "I guess I'll call him tomorrow."

"That negro should have died along with his new wife," Diamond shot back.

Nicole and I jerked our heads towards her as our mouths dropped. "I'm going to pretend that's the alcohol talking Diamond. Don't talk like that. Don't stoop to that level sweetie." She rolled her eyes and proceeded to focus in on her drink.

"I need a fucking nut after this uncomfortable encounter." I pulled out my cell phone and began to go through potential smash buddies. I came across a familiar name. Someone I hadn't talked to in a few weeks. "Hmm Head Hunter!"

Diamond looked at me and laughed, "Girl you ain't called Paul since you had that negro crying outside your door. How dare you make that boy go out the back?" Diamond was falling over laughing and my girls Jessica and Tanya joined in.

Nicole nudged me and said, "Hell try it. As good as you used to describe him it'll be worth the turn down. I mean that's if he turns you down."

"Wait why aren't you texting your boo Denim?" Jessica asked.

I rolled my eyes. I didn't want to discuss why Denim wasn't the first I would call. It was the weekend and I knew he was out anyway. Out with whom I don't know but I was sure it was with some woman. "I don't want to come off clingy. I just saw him."

"Clingy?" They all yelled in unison.

"How the hell are you clingy to your man?" Diamond asked.

"He isn't my man," I shot back.

Nicole shook her head in confusion and laughed out, "How the hell are you two claiming y'all in love and all this crap and y'all not together."

"Y'all don't have to understand," I said waving them off. I selected Paul's number and text him.

Hey

"Yeah we don't understand," Diamond shot back taking a sip of her drink.

"It's easier to not have titles. To just allow things to flow," I preached again.

"Who are you trying to convince us or you?" Nicole asked. The other ladies gave each other a high five in agreement.

"Change the subject," I dryly replied. When I felt my phone buzz I looked down to see a pending message.

Hey You!

I smiled, squeezing my legs really tight. "Doesn't matter what y'all say now anyway. I have some pending dick waiting. Ciao!" I grabbed my purse and headed for the exit texting Paul at the same time making sure our session was confirmed.

***

I walked around my house making sure everything was in its place. The setting was dark and alluring. I made sure I spread cherry's blossom all over my body giving that sweet scent Paul would always fall for.

I had taken a quick shave, trimming my kitty, and leaving a baby smooth surface across my legs. I placed on a silk nighty that complemented my already silky skin and sat down on the edge of my bed.

I heard two soft knocks on my door and a purr escaped my mouth. I was so excited to get assaulted in the best way that my kitty's pearl tongue was struggling to stay in between my lips. "Coming," I called out slipping out of my house shoes so that I could open my door bare foot.

"Hey you."

I moaned, biting my bottom lip at the sight of Paul. Mr. Head Hunter himself was here in my space alive and very well endowed.

"Hey to you too," he grunted, walking in my doorway and bringing me into his arms. "Hmm you smell good."

I smiled, burying my nose in his neck. I was more than excited to have him here. We hadn't seen each other since that awkward Denim moment.

"Come on inside. Make yourself comfortable."

Paul passed me as I closed the door and proceeded to unzip his jacket and toss it across my couch. "Bring your sexy ass on," he ordered.

I tried to hide my excitement and match his serious stare. I loved being ordered around in the bedroom. Paul knew just how to please me so maybe that's why it was so hard to get him out of my system. Then I laughed at the thought. Ha like that will ever happened. I mean why not have fun? Denim never asked me to be his girl so therefore I was free to do what I wanted. And I did. Two times.

Claire

"It's like you're caught up in a maze and keep going in circles and you're trying to find a way out. But I'm stuck in the middle trying to figure out which way to go."

I was at a lunch outing with Diamond, Nicole, Tanya, and Janet. We had met up at Twin Peaks for drinks and appetizers and I had to come clean about my torn affection.

"I want to make it work," I added.

"But do you really? Why even get caught up in this Lewis guy anyway?" Diamond asked.

"If you saw him you would understand why I was drawn in but then I started talking to him. And that's when everything started to change."

"Whelp first mistake boo. First of all, if you're trying to be like me you can't be talking to a negro, cupcaking on the phone, and all that jazz. You have to know how to limit your communication," Janet blurted.

"I don't want to be like you," I shot back.

"What, free?"

"No confused," I blurted. A few of the girls laughed.

"Excuse me I am not confused. I am just free to do as I choose."

"Girl you do as you choose simply because Denim's ass is. You ain't fooling anyone," Nicole added.

"I was this way before Denim."

Diamond held up her hands to interject. "Okay y'all get off my baby sister now okay? Sure she was this way before Denim, but baby girl you have gotten worse and I think it's because you truly love that man."

THE 🖤 I Didn't Say

I imagined my sisters were insinuating the string of one night stands I have had in the last month. Many of whom I met at grocery stores, lounges, or a gas station. I would sex them and send them on their merry way. I was becoming a true bed crusher in the worst way attempting to bury my feelings for Denim.

"Yep I agree," I added.

"Okay so yeah I do love him but he ain't ready."

"What and you are?" Tanya asked. We all looked over to Janet and studied her waiting on her answer.

"I don't know. I mean if he was then I would be."

"See that's where you are wrong Janet. You got to be ready because you are, not because of the decisions he is making. So in that case baby girl you ain't ready," I preached.

"Well I'm going to have to agree with Claire on that one," Diamond added.

"Me too," Nicole and Tanya said in unison.

I waved them off. "Whatever, hell why be with one man anyway. They will never be with just one woman."

Diamond interjected, "Now that I sort of agree with as well and it's not because men are dogs either."

"Then why?" I asked curiously wondering why my own husband had a wandering eye.

"Women make it easy. It's like men don't know how to wine and dine or woo a woman anymore because he doesn't have to. Women are throwing the coochie at them via text, Facebook inbox, email, hell, probably the postal service too. Mr. Post Man probably is getting cooch on a regular with how hungry these hoes are. Even the greatest man can falter when a bare cooch is sitting in his face and he doesn't have to work for it. Hell I would take up that offer if I knew I wouldn't get caught."

I stared at Diamond giving her philosophy on men and asked, "So what do we do?"

She waved me off. "Girl ain't shit you can do but hope and pray your man ain't a weak one. Let's hope and pray we all get a man who knows that a few pumps in the rump ain't worth a lifetime of pain once she walks away."

"I don't even see why people even get married. Did y'all know forty percent of people are cheating with married men anyway?" Tanya asked.

We all asked, "Where did you hear that from?"

"Being Mary Jane, that show on BET. Girl they are giving the real shit on that show."

I sighed and rolled my eyes. "Another show where the main character is the side piece. Oh okay."

Tanya shrugged. "What? It makes for good TV. "Hell our life is aa reality show in itself, who would need to watch it on TV?

I took a bite of my turkey wrap and asked, "So I should end it with Lewis?"

Janet shot out, "Nope. We both know Evan's ass is on some bull any way. Go have fun girl. Hell all of our men have cheated or will cheat. I am starting to really see that now."

I studied her and laughed. "Oh is that a jab towards Denim?"

She waved me off, "Whatever."

We sat and chatted for a little while longer until I told them that I had to go. They all eyed me as Diamond joked, "Go have fun with the doc bitch. We won't tell."

I waved them off and hugged them all before walking out and hopping in my BMW. I pulled out my cell and began to go through my contacts until I landed on Lewis' name. I pressed call.

He answered on the third ring. "Hey I was just thinking about you."

"You were?"

"I was. How is your day going so far beautiful?" I blushed when Lewis randomly complimented me. It was always the simple things Evan didn't do that always made me feel special.

"I just had lunch with my girls, now I am headed back to my office."

THE **I Didn't Say**

"Change those plans and make your way here. I go to lunch in a few it would be nice to see you." I smiled brightly, excited that he did exactly what I called for. I wanted to see him.

I didn't want to do much but just to sit in front of him, to be in his presence, to feel appreciated and noticed.

"I'm on my way. See you in a bit." I pressed the end button just as my phone buzzed in my hand. I looked down to see who was calling. Evan.

I decided to answer now so that he wouldn't call later. "Hey," I said dryly.

"Well hello to you too. Where are you?"

"Having lunch with the girls in Midtown. What's up, everything okay?"

"Of course everything is okay. I am just calling to talk to my wife. Is that okay with you?"

I placed my car in reverse and rolled my eyes hoping he didn't hear me breathe out a sigh of annoyance. "Sure you can. So what's up?"

"So our guys here at the lot went way over the required quota this month babe, looks like I can upgrade you to that car you have always wanted."

I rolled my eyes, "That's great your guys did good. Happy for you." I said, yielding over into my left lane to get on highway 285.

"Umm okay. That's great news for us babe."

Call me crazy but Evan was being just a little bit too nice for me at this moment. He sounds genuine, actually offering up some dialogue and now he wants to get me a new car. Yeah, I wasn't crazy he was smartening up. The jig was up. I wasn't any fool either. My routine had changed. I smirked and looked at myself in my overhead mirror. I even looked different.

"Yeah it is great news babe." I put a little more sarcasm in the word babe. Since when does this negro call me babe?

"How long will you be out with the girls? I want to show you a few of the car selections we got on the lot."

"Well, I'm headed to one of three meetings right now so I'll let you know," I shot back.

"You'll let me know?" It wasn't as if he was asking me but I think he was trying to make sure that's what he heard.

"Yeah pretty busy day sir. So umm I'll call you later, cool?" Dead silence. I looked at my phone to see if he had hung up on me but he hadn't so I continued, "Hello!"

"Yeah Claire. I'll talk to you later."

"Okie dokie." I clicked the phone off before he could say another word and exited the highway headed for Lewis's office. I was really excited to see him. I'm gonna make sure I get at least three kisses. Okay okay maybe four.

Janet

I was a little annoyed sitting here at the bar a lone waiting on someone I had no interest in seeing. Seeing him once was enough. I trailed my finger across the base of my glass and eyed my apple martini. The drinks I had at lunch with the girls weren't enough. I needed a double shot of their strongest alcohol for this.

Bar Eleven was a pretty simple intimate bar. It was located south of downtown near some of the prettiest lofts the city had. An area I eyed once for living. I smiled briefly at the bartender who was eyeing me. I don't know if he were being nosey because I was sitting alone and watching me down this drink quicker than I should be.

"Hey Janet."

I cringed at the sound of Desmond's voice and turned in my bar stool to face him. "Desmond," I responded dryly.

"You look casually nice today." He took off his jacket and threw it on the back of his seat.

I brushed my hands over my hair pulling a few loose curls behind my ear and said, "Thanks. So I didn't order you anything. Because I didn't order you anything," I said rudely.

Laughing he said, "Going right on in aren't we."

I smirked. "Sure why not."

He turned to the bartender and ordered his liquor and a basket of fries and turned his attention back towards me. "Thank you for meeting with me."

"Sure I'm just that nice of a gal to sit next to the man I hadn't seen in years. Oh who so happened to have done the unthinkable to me. But sure the pleasure is all mine. How are you by the way?"

Desmond's mouth was slightly parted as he stared at me in what looked like shock. I guess I was coming off as a bitter bitch. I made a mental note to take it down a notch. Don't let this man see that he is getting to you.

"Umm okay. I'm okay, thanks for asking."

I tried to lighten up the mood. "What are you in Atlanta for now? When did you leave Philadelphia?"

"I left about a year ago. I am actually thinking about moving here."

It took all of my might not to roll my eyes. I would hate to know he was in the same city as me. "Oh okay. So you wanted to meet. So go on and spill it." I was hoping that he would get straight to the point the limit the amount of time I had to be seated in front of him.

Taking a sip of his drink the bartender sat before him he laughed, "Still the same Janet."

"Exactly, I never changed."

"Straight to the point?"

"Straight like that!" I now took a sip of my drink and then clasped my hands together giving him my undivided attention.

"After the accident, it took me several months to get back to this. I wasn't what you see today. It was when I first began to get well that I asked about you."

"So you didn't ask about your wife?"

There was an awkward pause. "They had told me upon wakening that she had died on impact. I chose to not think about her to be able to function."

"So they told you about her but not your girlfriend of five years. Ooookkkkay that makes no sense. So everyone knew about her?"

"Yes, everyone knew of her for about a year. It wasn't supposed to be that deep but it happened. One day we just went and got married."

"Did she know about me?"

He shook his head no. I dropped my head making my drink my new focus. I don't even know why I was entertaining this

113

with one hundred and one questions. This wasn't helping me, it was making my blood boil and doing more harm.

"They told me you had come to the hospital and that the very next day you had my best friend come and get all of my things from the house."

"As he should have."

"Even on my death bed you felt nothing?"

"What was I supposed to do? Be your wife since the one you married died? Umm no!" I heard the words come out of my mouth after saying it and felt bad. I mean she didn't do anything wrong, he did and I didn't feel sorry for his situation. Karma was a bitch. That's how I felt.

"No, I am not saying that Janet."

"Okay look, I see what you mean. I was supposed to react some type of way when you were hurt. By your definition I should have been more caring right?" I signaled towards him to answer.

"Yeah something like that."

"See that's where we don't agree. You lying in that bed didn't change the fact that you didn't care enough about me. It didn't change the fact that you stole my youth and then went to marry someone else. So now I guess this is the moment I ask you: why?" I was no holds barred right now. I kind of felt proud of myself. Here I sat across from a man who tore a major hole in my heart and I was literally ripping a new hole in his.

"I guess you're right."

I laughed to myself. See men kill me. There is something I guess a man and woman will never understand about each other. A man can take you through so much. Break your heart over and over again, give you false promises, break your trust, sleep with every woman up under the sun and still expect us to be there by their side. And when that woman is strong enough not to tolerate the bullshit doesn't stand by him then we're the ones that are wrong.

Call me crazy. You know what, don't call me crazy. Call me a genius not to be dumb enough to be someone's doormat. I deserve more.

Women deserve more than to settle for sharing their man. Say for instance we decide to treat him the way he has treated us that negro is on the next train moving and there's no take backs. A man will never forgive a woman for doing a mere fraction of the dirt he has done.

"You can't expect me to be there for you after you broke my heart. Don't you think that's a tad selfish?"

"You never gave me a chance to explain," he shot back.

"I didn't need an explanation Desmond. It was written on a Georgia issued marriage license." I threw up my hands in frustration. "You're killing me here."

"Why are you so hard?"

It was in that moment I looked at Desmond differently. Paul had asked me that same question, and so did Kelvin, Tony, Eric, Steven, Adam, Lytrell, Mike, Tone, ooo that guy from the car wash, Pete, Gerald, what's his name from the lounge last year, Isaiah, Frank, the bouncer from Krave, and oh yeah the cute guy I dated for a month his name started with a D I think.

My attempting to recall my memory must have been written all over my face as Desmond asked me was I ok. "I've been asked that before," I replied.

"What?"

"Why am I so hard?"

There was another long awkward silence. "It's because of me right?"

I nodded my head yes. "I never wanted someone for something they had. I simply wanted to have a partner, a best friend, someone who understood my soul. I thought I had that in you. I could sit here and act hard like I don't give a damn but I do. You did hurt me. So yeah explain that."

"I started to change Janet. We fell in love as kids and somewhere down the line we both began to grow and change. I wasn't the same and I actually couldn't handle your career. After you began writing, it wasn't just us anymore."

"My career pushed you away?"

"I admired what you did, believe that, but I was selfish. We never did the things that we used to do anymore. It always had to wait until you met a deadline, or finished research, or you had to travel to this event and so on."

I shook my head and said, "Okay that's it?"

He looked at me confused and frowned, "What do you mean that's it?"

"I was still fucking you, I wasn't cheating, damn near cooked every day, was bringing in so much money I was helping you launch your dream. Must I go on?"

He stared at me speechless. Ten seconds passed. Then ten more and he finally said, "Sounds like I was ungrateful."

I laughed and downed the rest of my drink. "I was a good woman. And I let you change me."

I didn't wait for him to respond. I grabbed my purse and marched out of the bar. I didn't look back as he called my name. Besides I had given him five years and this sorry ass excuse of a conversation. I wasn't going to waste another breath on him.

Denim

I moaned, stretching my limbs in an effort to release some of the tension my shoulders were giving out. It wasn't even eight in the morning yet and I was awake. I blew out a breath of annoyance turning my face when I smelled my morning breath. I grunted and looked over to my right and noticed a head full of hair.

What the hell!

She lay turning the opposite way showing her bare. I sized her up, looking at her shapely hips covered by a mere sheet; her waist line was nearly nonexistent and led to a curvy rump. I bit my bottom lip and stared at her ass and tried to recall last night's activities.

She is sexy as hell!

I reached back trying to move as slowly as I could without waking her to grab my phone. I felt the beginning or a raging headache when I saw the amount of texts and missed calls from various people. I skimmed through and noticed Janet called and text a few times. Her last attempt was at eight o'clock.

It's damn near twelve hours later. I tried to think of the last time we spoke. I think I was at lunch. Now my headache grew as I knew that I was going to be interrogated by Janet about why she hadn't heard from me in damn near a day.

I put my phone back deciding to text her in an hour when I felt the touch of someone's hand on my back. "Hmmm good morning D," she purred.

"Good morning." Looking at her face for the first time since awakening I was more than pleased. This woman was beautiful. Now it made sense on why I brought her home.

THE ▓▓▓ I Didn't Say

She leaned in and kissed me on the neck. I nuzzle her head on my chest and wrapped my arm around her waist allowing her to get more comfortable next to me.

"Baby you smell good." She smiled and thanked me. I didn't know shorty's name. But honestly half of the time I didn't know any of their names so I called them common pet names.

I felt the rise of her cheeks pressed against my chest insinuating she loved my complimenting her. She slowly began to kiss my chest and looking down I saw the reaction to her touch stand straight up under the covers.

"Hmmm papi are you excited to see me this morning?" She eyed my hardness and purred. I got a good glimpse of her face. She's exotic looking maybe Puerto Rican.

I shook my head yes as I pushed my head back into my pillow and released my hold of her waist. She moved lower and lower, kiss by kiss, and inch by inch she was about to speak into the mic. I felt the tips of my toes curl as I knew I was about to feed her morning breakfast.

After pulling back the covers she moaned. I watched the arch in her eyebrows as she bit her bottom lip and smiled. "DJ Denim O has a gorgeous dick!" I loved her Spanish tongue.

I thank her as she grabbed me by the waist, leaning downward directing my head to land on her lips. I was so turned on by the slurps and gagging sounds she was making that I grabbed the back of her head to guide the pace.

She moved her mouth slowly then quickly sucked and pulling on my flesh. Maintaining my erection in the morning wasn't always an easy task and I didn't fight what was the inevitable. My seeds spewing in her mouth I blew out a deep breath and complimented her on her skills.

I rolled over to hop in the shower and asked her to join me in hopes to making this a quick exit so that I could get to my messages.

I had Ms. Puerto Rican showered, dressed, and out my front door within forty-five minutes. Throwing myself across my bed I grabbed my cell to see a few fresh messages. I ignored them all and skimmed to see if Janet had sent something new. When I saw an alert by her name I knew that she had to have sent something. I just know she's going to ask me where I have been all this time.

Her messages read:

I'd cut my soul into a million different pieces just to form a constellation to light your way home. I'd write love poems to the parts of yourself you can't stand. I'd stand in the shadows of your heart and tell you I'm not afraid of your dark.

-Andrea Gibson

I was so blindsided by those words that I had to read it again. And then I read it again and just stared at them. "Wow!" sprung from my mouth and echoed around my empty bedroom.

I took to my keyboard and text back;

Wow that was beautiful.

In seconds her name popped up with the message;

Morning Mr. Beautiful just thought I would share how I was feeling this morning.

I smiled and asked her what she was doing today. I wanted to see her in the worst way. Wait. Why wasn't she interrogating me? This was just too…wait what is this? Perfect; right this is just too perfect. Something is up. I text:

What's up, how was your morning? Is everything ok?

Janet: Everything is ok my love, let's meet up tonight. Dinner, my treat?

Your treat, ok woman are you trying to woo me?

Janet: LOL very funny. But I think I am already accomplishing that. Eight tonight at Houstons in Buckhead. Deal?

Deal. Muah.

Janet: Muahhhhh Muah

I hopped up and dressed quickly to head into my office wanting to get some work done before I saw Janet tonight. I did still feel weird though that she seemed cool to not have heard from me all of these hours. Then it all made sense, she's out there doing

THE 𝗙𝗨𝗖𝗞 I Didn't Say

her thing just like I am doing mine. Hell, she probably had a man in her bed last night.

I loved Janet and all but she proved to me every day that we were one and the same and if I couldn't trust me, then I damn well for sure couldn't trust her. I knew what I was capable of. I could break a heart and if Janet was like me, then that meant it was only a matter of time before she would break mines. At least that's how it works right? You live, you love, you get hurt. Repeated bullshit at its finest.

Janet

I studied my phone for what seemed like hours but was only minutes. I hadn't heard from Denim in damn near twelve hours. He had a busy schedule but he always sent texts throughout the day. I would be lying if I said I didn't notice his absence, that I wish I wasn't thinking about whose bed was he in last night.

But I had to shake those thoughts out of my head. Yeah it was obvious that he was with someone simply because he was MIA. I bit my tongue though. Realistically I can't get mad or question him. We agreed on no strings, just have fun. Funny thing is we were doing the complete opposite of just having fun. We had fallen for each other.

I was jealous though, don't get me wrong. I was jealous of her, the woman who got to spend time with him instead of me. I could have called someone to fill his space but I was beginning to get tired of that. I didn't want to bury my feelings for him with some random guy. I just wanted him.

Finally rolling out of my bed I allow my feet to hang off the side hitting the wooden frame as I took my time to rise. Working for myself sometimes can be crippling simply because I create my own schedule. Today was a prime example of how I wanted to be lazy and didn't have any pressure to be anything else but that. Being lazy meant no work got done and I couldn't have that.

I walk into my bathroom planting myself in front of the mirror. I hadn't slept in past nine in the morning in weeks and it felt different, it felt good to just be for a moment. I stared at my plain face. Emotionless, make up free, and simple. I couldn't help

THE ██ I Didn't Say

but to smile back at my reflection. I was in a good place now. I felt that I was going to get everything right and that was finally getting Denim to see that he and I should be in a commitment. .

But of course I couldn't come out right and say it. I needed to make him see it through my actions. I walked into my closet and eyed the salmon colored sundress I bought from the boutique on Peachtree in midtown and decided I would wear that. I matched it with golden sandals, a few loose bracelets, and my gold hoop earrings.

After taking a shower I curled my hair, lotioned my entire body, and dressed. I made a quick stop at the floral shop around the corner from my house and bought a single violet. Hopping on the freeway I made my way to work and later on off to Buckhead I couldn't even hide the smile that spread wide across my cheeks that resemble pink rose petals at this moment. I was excited. I was anxious. Anxious for what, I didn't quite know yet.

€€€

The hours didn't pass fast enough as I walked into Houston's dimly lit restaurant and asked the hostess for a table for two. I had managed to get there before him so that I could be seated at the table first.

I was attracted to the fact that Denim was almost always on time. When he said he was going to be there; he usually was there on time. Crossing my legs underneath the table I push backwards into my chair and wait.

"Hey beautiful." The corners of my mouth rose into the biggest smile seeing Denim walk up towards me. I stood up hugging him and lastly giving him a familiar kiss on the cheek.

"You look handsome." I complimented him on his casual but handsome attire. He smelled good, like he stepped out of a fresh shower. His beard and hair was freshly cut, and I eyed his hands. I loved a man with clean nails and smooth hands. Denim's hands were the definition of what I liked.

"You look beautiful babe. How was your day?"

122

I reached down in my seat and pulled out the violet and smiled, "It was great!"

He eyed the flower and I just about melted. Men weren't used to receiving flowers. I decided against the single red rose and to do something a tad bit different. As chocolate as Denim was his cheeks were a misty red as if a dash of blush was laced across his face.

"You like?" I asked. My smile as bright as it could ever be. My eyes were lit and my heart seemed to be beating its way through my chest. I don't know why I was nervous. I don't know why I felt like this was our first date. I had known him for months now.

He laughed and reached for it. "Babe you are always doing something."

I laughed back, "Doing what? Making you smile." I pushed upward out of my seat and leaned over the table to kiss him. "Kiss me!" I ordered.

He leaned forward and kissed me back. I loved his full lips on top of mine. I loved it more when he studied my lips in between our kisses. I loved it when it seemed that our bodies became one just from a kiss.

"Thanks babe, what's it for?"

"No reason," I said, causally popping a piece of bread in my mouth. "Order whatever you want on the menu."

"So what do you have for me?" He asked curiously raising an eyebrow.

I shrugged my shoulders and teased, "I figured why not feed the big baby and be nice for once."

"Big baby huh? We'll see who's calling who a big baby."

"When and where because I want to be in the front row for this," I shot back.

"You are the row babe. You'll be every bit of the main showpiece I promise you."

I laughed, throwing my head back allowing my laugh to echo off the walls of the restaurant. It wasn't that he was the funniest guy it was the mere fact that it was him. "It's all about you tonight D, order whatever it is that you want."

"Ooookkkkay I am going to order the most expensive thing on the menu."

I wink and shrugged my shoulders adding on the fact that I would match his price. "How was work today, what did you do?"

I wasn't too wrapped up into the music industry and didn't understand how it all worked but Denim and I were both artists. We were passionate, obsessive, weird beings and we understood that about each other. So my asking him about his work wasn't for me it was for him because just like any other artists we need to express our artistry. To get it out and hope that it all makes sense because our minds are constantly running.

"I worked with a new jazz artist for a track my hip hop artist is working on."

"You like jazz though?" I asked curiously because I for one loved it.

"Oh yeah my mom use to listen to the sounds of Blossom Dearie and Abbey Lincoln. Ever heard of Betty Carter?"

I shook my head no. "She sang jazz too?"

"Yeah she's one of my favorites. I like to go to San Francisco a lot to just enjoy the wineries, the many restaurants and places where they play live music. It's the city of love for me. I love it there."

I shrugged my shoulders. "Never been. Maybe I'll go."

"Hmmm maybe I'll take you then."

"Hmmm that would be nice." I took a sip of my red wine and eyed him. "You look really nice tonight Denim."

"You look really nice tonight as well Janet."

Once our food arrived I listened to him explain to me his days' work. I later went into telling him about my current ghostwriting project. I didn't notice a staring eye until my spirit told me to pay attention. I felt as if someone wouldn't allow me to just be in this moment.

I turned my head to see what this feeling was coming from when Denim blurted, "So this project of yours when will it be done?"

Turning my attention back to him I took a swallow of my food and replied, "In about a month hopefully."

I was distracted by the one hundred and one questions he was asking me now and soon enough just ignored that eerie feeling and gave him all of my attention.

Denim

I stepped into Houston's exhausted. I had worked for the past seven hours on various tracks for my artist and only came out with one hit. I actually should have stayed in for the night but I didn't want to disappoint Janet. I had cancelled the last few times for us to actually have a date and I didn't want to do that this time. I needed a break from the studio.

Dalvin was in Texas visiting his kids and I was missing a piece of home myself. So much so I was this close to telling Nitrah to bring her ass back into town. But I didn't want to seem stingy. I suppose if I was missing something that made me feel like home then I would need to be with Janet tonight. She was beginning to be that for me.

I was still adjusting to these feelings. I actually liked her. Then I actually loved her. And lastly I always wanted to talk to her or be around her but that wasn't always enough when it came to us. We are a couple who is difficult and I for one was selfish. I still didn't want to have to answer to anyone. Not even Janet.

Walking in I had to take a deep breath. It was crazy how sometimes when I saw Janet it was as if I was seeing her for the first time. My heart fluttered so much that I thought it was noticeable and I would subconsciously look down to see if you could see it beating through my shirt.

She was beautiful simply because she was Janet. I was addicted to her and I didn't know why. I just loved who she was. I loved her smile. I loved her laugh. I loved the way her hair curled behind her ears and how when she felt self-conscious she would pull it back making a tight c around her ears with her hair. I noticed her. I noticed when she was sad, when she was mad, when something bothered her, and even when she was happy or excited. I knew her. I felt her. Often times we just knew what was going on in each other's head.

"You look beautiful babe," I said, sitting down. I noticed Janet smile brightly and pull a violet from beneath the table.

I dropped my head slightly to hide my bashful smile and readjusted myself. I was blown by how this woman always knew how to make me smile.

"Thanks babe you are something else." She leaned over and kissed my lips. I welcome her full lips. I often called them pillows because I could find myself wanting to just stay planted there. Right on her lips. I could make a home there.

When she took a seat I looked over her right shoulder and locked eyes with Lena. Tilting my head awkwardly I eyed her and frowned. What the hell was she doing here?

Now wasn't the time to be acting out. I didn't want this woman to ruin my mood or better yet my situation with Janet. I was comfortable and that meant I had neglected some of the ladies on my roster; that included Lena. I hadn't spent time with her in weeks, she was actually just my assistant now and each and every time she had a chance she tried to have sex.

"D; are you okay?" Janet asked mere seconds from turning her head to see what it was that I was looking at.

I allowed the words to spew out of my mouth, "Yeah babe I'm fine. Thanks for the flower." I sat it on the seat next to me and studied Janet. In my mind I did not want her to look back. If she looked back this wouldn't end to well. She knew Lena's face; she knew I used to fuck her. She knew it all.

"I wanted to try this chilled salmon on the appetizer menu. They serve it with saltine crackers. Ever had that?" She asked.

I shook my head no. "Let's try it. I am also in the mood for some steak." I tried to force calmness in my tone. I was hoping that it was working.

"You look tense. How was work, tell me about it?"

I smiled. Not because she said something special but because of what she said. There has never been a woman who has

THE **I Didn't Say**

asked me about my day and actually wanted to know the answer. Not anyone since Nitrah and Janet often asked. And I knew that she meant it because she had follow up questions. She was actually interested.

So I began to tell her about my day. It was the moments like this when we were just being us that I enjoyed. I in turn always asked her about her day. Sometimes her clients were difficult and I wanted her to vent to me. I never actually cared to listen to a woman complain or confide in me. That would mean that I cared. But I did with her.

In the corner of my eye I could still see Lena. She watched every move that we made. I grew impatient with this awkward situation. What is she doing here? Maybe I could just ask Janet for us to leave but then she would want to know why.

"How about we get our food to go?" The words had escaped my mouth without much thought. I could only see the image in my head of Lena creating a scene and Janet being disappointed in me. It's not that I was afraid of being called out on some dirt. It was the mere fact that some things I just didn't want Janet to know.

"Why, what's wrong?" Janet reached over and placed her hand on mine which lay still on the table.

"It's been a long day and I would rather spend the rest of the night a lone. Your place is cool?"

"Yeah okay we can do that." She reached in her purse for her wallet as I raise up my hand to stop her.

"Go on to your car and I'll meet you at the house. I got the bill."

Janet began to sulk with concern. "Babe is something wrong, what's going on?"

"Babe I got this. Nothing is wrong. I'm just tired. A little agitated with the idea that I am not somewhere alone with you right now. That's where I would rather be."

She smiled brightly at me while sliding from behind the table and standing up to retrieve her purse. "I'll see you in a little while okay?" She leaned over me and kissed me softly as I nod my head okay. I followed her silhouette as she made her way out of the restaurant and when she was gone I turned my head and jumped.

"What the fuck?" Lena had come from nowhere and was now seated in the same spot Janet had just left. "What the hell are you doing?"

"You in a little while." Lena leaned back in her seat and smirked.

"What are you even doing here? Are you following me?"

She raised an eyebrow and rolled her eyes. "I was here before you babe. Duhh. Now why would I follow you like some stalker?"

"I don't know why would you be seating across from me as if my girl wasn't just right here?"

She gave out a soft chuckle and clasped her hands together. "Oh now she's your girl. Boy please. You will never be with one woman. She knows that right?"

"Knows what?" My voice was stern and low. I was growing impatient with this conversation.

"That you're an untrainable whore."

I heard a voice come from behind me that nearly scared me into an irregular heartbeat. "Are you dining in with us ma'am?" It was my server coming back to check on our table.

I quickly interjected. "Can you wrap up this appetizer and the food my lady and I ordered and bring me the check?" The server quickly agreed and scurried off to get our food. I was hoping that it was quick so that I could get away from Lena.

I watched her. Studying even the way her chest rose and fell with every breath. Lena was very tempting to say the least but I couldn't go there with her anymore. She, like most of the women I slept with, had started to expect things from me.

She placed her arms to her sides as if she was using them for leverage and began to sink lower into her seat. "I've missed you Big D."

I studied her unmoved and as I attempted to ask her to leave again I felt the initial touch of her feet on my leg. I flinched and frowned at her. "Don't Lena."

"Don't what?" She playfully asked.

"Move!" I attempted to kick away her leg with my leg but that didn't stop her persistence.

"Babe I've missed you." Her voice was low and husky. I knew she was going to try me right now. Lena didn't take no for an answer when it came to sex. One thing I could always count on her was being my promiscuous girl. She did any and everything I wanted whenever I wanted. And in this moment that very characteristic had me nervous. I knew if there was any way of shutting her attempts down I had to do it now and fast.

"Have you missed me?" She asked trailing her feet up my leg and now my inner thigh. I was in a losing battle. I felt myself harden with just the touch of her feet there. Then she began to tease my zipper. I knew she felt my hardness. She saw the fight within my eyes to show face and to look unmoved but that wasn't working. She knew she had me.

She purred, "Hmm Daddy's dick is happy to see me!"

I eyed her with my eyes pleading with her to stop but we have played this game before. She was turned on by the mere fact that I wanted her to stop. I dropped my head quickly to regroup and as I attempted to reface her she had disappeared.

I began to look to my left and then to my right. What the hell? Am I tripping? I jerked at the first initial touch. She's under the table.

I began to search my surroundings and look for any signs of the server. My hands frantically went each and every way under the table pushing Lena backwards but my efforts to do it subtle wasn't making any impact. I was losing as I felt her hands rummage over my belt buckle. "Woman stop!" I said in between grunted teeth.

"Why?" Was all she said.

It was as if an electric current shot through my body at the obvious question of why. Why was I stopping her from doing what we both wanted her to do anyway? Maybe it was a slight sense of a desire to change, to want something different. Or maybe it was the fear that Janet would walk back in and see me doing the unthinkable. For her this would be the unthinkable. For me this was just another day with Lena. My weakness.

In the seconds I stood still thinking of her question of why Lena had manage to unzip my pants was now lathering my hardness with the wetness of her mouth. I felt myself tighten up at the intense affect she was having over me. I loved a woman who could take control. A woman who went after what it was that she wanted. And Lena wanted nothing more for me to be in her mouth. For my seeds to spill over and drizzle down her throat.

I was failing at this test and I didn't even care. I clinch my ass and pushed my hips upward forcing myself deeper into her mouth. It was warm and cool as I discovered she had ice in her mouth. I whence and moaned allowing my head to fall back as my eyes closed.

"Sir your bill." My eyes jerked open as I locked eyes with my server who handed me the bill. Weak from the intense pleasure I was receiving underneath the table I quickly grabbed for it missing it at my first attempt but connecting my hand with the folder on the second.

"I...I...I got it. Thankssss. That. That will be all."

"Your food is at the bar sir." She stopped and raised a curious eyebrow. "Are you okay sir?"

"Yes, I am fine." I shook my head like it was dangling off of loose wire and encouraged her to leave my table.

Lena had now placed her hands on my hip bone and with no hands she moved up and down faster and swifter. I felt like I was inside of her. The mere fact of getting caught cause my emotions to run wild. My toes curled and I could feel the initial sensation of my seeds spewing like a blocked ketchup refusing to come out of its container and then suddenly without warning it spilled over.

THE 🞄🞄🞄 I Didn't Say

"Ahhhh. I grunted." I grabbed the back of her head so that she would be stuck in place as I felt the warm liquid ooze its way onto her hot tongue. I felt my eyes mist as I went to wipe them with the back of my hand. I could feel Lena move away from me as I hurriedly went to zip up my pants.

My eyes searched my surroundings again and no one even noticed our under the table sexcapades. I pulled out my wallet and dropped several bills on the table without counting and scooted out of the booth. Rushing towards the door I didn't even look back to see where Lena now was. I didn't care. I needed to get away from her and quickly.

€€€

I walked into Janet's house. I heard the sounds of Will Downing dancing through the air as I placed our food on her kitchen table. "Babe!" I called out.

I heard her in the back calling out that she would be right up. I had a key to her home now because we made a habit of always being in each other's space she wanted to make it easier for me to just come over. So letting myself in was easy. I however never used her key without letting her know I was on my way. I on the other hand haven't extended that invitation to my house.

I hope she didn't do that just to get a reaction out of me. "The place looks nice." I hadn't been over in a couple weeks but I noticed a new couch, some exotic paintings, and some statuettes she now had in her living space.

Janet walked in wearing simple shorts that barely covered her ass and one of the white t shirts I often wore underneath my shirts. "Really babe you're going to come out looking like that teasing me?"

She looked down and her eyes traveled from one erect nipple to another and smirked. "Whatever do you mean babe?" She laughed. I laughed. She walked over to me and kissed my lips and began to go through the food. "I hope you didn't mess up the order D, you know you do that a lot."

132

"I know, I know."

"It's you and always having these assistants does everything for you. How about tomorrow I show you how to go grocery shopping?"

"Grocery shopping? What do I need to know that for?"

"To be self-sufficient babe. You should be more hands on," she said, placing a piece of her steak in her mouth. "Come on and sit down. I'll go grab two glasses of wine.

I did as I was told and took a seat at the table separating our food to her liking. In the middle of my setting the table I observed the routine of it all. I was in a relationship without saying I was in a relationship. I shook those thoughts out of my head and waited for Janet to come back with the wine. I needed a drink or two.

"Okay so is this better, you look more relaxed," Janet said sitting my glass in front of me.

I raised an eyebrow as the memory of Lena's mouth on me began to resurface. I felt myself jerk in my pants. I shook my head shamefully at just how my body reacted to the thought of that woman. Who was I fooling, I loved women. I loved everything about them. Their breasts, their small hands, the curve of their lower back that led to a plump round booty. Mmmm. I didn't notice I moaned out loud until Janet said, "Geesh hungry aren't we?"

"Ummm yeah I've been waiting on this. Say grace so we can eat." We bowed our heads and closed our eyes as Janet led the grace.

"What do you want to do after this?" Janet asked.

"Honestly nothing. We bought that DVD last week and we still haven't watched it."

"So you wanna do that? That's fine. I could use a break from writing. Tomorrow though Nicole asked us to come to a mixer event with Essence Magazine. It's like honoring women in photography or something of that nature. She's one of the honorees."

"No shit?"

THE ⬛ I Didn't Say

"No shit." She laughed. "I said that too. My baby sis is growing up and making moves. Proud of her. So you want to go?"

"Yeah babe I'll go and show Nicole some support. Maybe I should throw her some work. I am working with Usher's protégé and they are looking to get some early media exposure. Plus I have some connects over at TVOne."

"You are something else." Janet rose up from her seat and walked over towards me. Once she was standing beside me I allow myself to look up to her and smile.

"You are beautiful babe."

Her smile was infectious. She stood so close to me I could feel her breath escape from her mouth and onto my cheeks. Her eyes were glowing, brightly with genuine love. I could see the love in her eyes. It was very evident that she had allowed me in. In many ways I had allowed her in too.

"Thanks." She managed to speak before softly kissing me on my lips. She pushed me back into my seat and straddled me. Our kiss deepened. I wasn't normally a kisser and when I did kiss the person on the opposite end would be Janet. I couldn't completely enjoy this moment as I kept thinking of the evidence that still lay within my boxer briefs.

Janet

I think his lips were made for me. I think his kiss was made to just kiss me. It had to be the reason for what I was feeling right now. His kiss. Ugh how I loved his kiss. I loved the fullness of his mouth on mine. We both had full big plump lips and it sometimes seemed that we were fighting for space. My bottom lip in between his, then his top lip covering mine, then my tongue flicking his lips as he bites mine. Hmmm we played with each other's mouths often. We kissed often but not like this. Not like what I was experiencing at this very moment.

Ever had a kiss so perfect that you didn't want it to end? So you grab the persons face and push them further into your mouth. You breathe deep. So deep that your chest caves in and as you exhale you release that breath into their mouth. With the travels of your breath comes along your soul and in that moment your soul is inside of them.

You can feel their heart beating from the inside. You can hear their thoughts and feel the blood running through their veins. You can simply feel them because you are now them. In one kiss you become one heart, one breath, one soul, you became each other.

I was now inside of Denim. I felt him so heavy that I shook at the mere touch of his hands traveling up and down my back. I could kiss him for an eternity and just be in this moment.

"I love you." I managed to say in between pecks.

"I love you more." He leaned back and stared at me as the words easily slipped through his lips. I smiled and just stared at him.

THE ![icon] I Didn't Say

I couldn't explain this moment. No words were spoken but so much was said. His eyes staring directly into mine and mine staring directly into his. I told him so much. I revealed my true feelings. I wanted to say that I changed my mind. That I only wanted him and that nobody else can give me what I get from him. How do I say it without scaring him off?

I opened my mouth to speak just as Denim leans in, kisses me quickly on the lips, and slaps my ass. "Dessert?"

"I...I...I have ice cream," I managed to say attempting to pull myself out of that trance. Now isn't the time anyway. It's too early to talk about commitment and all that jazz.

"That's it? I knew I should have gotten that chocolate cream filled cheesecake."

I stood up and asked, "You wanna go out for dessert or do you wanna watch the movie?" I grabbed our plastic ware and made a B line to the trash can to dispose of everything.

"No, let's just relax. We can go out afterwards."

Walking back in I smiled, "I knew you would say that. I mean when do we ever get to just rest?"

"Not too often. I mean I will rest starting next week."

I raised an eyebrow and tried to not sound upset or annoyed at what he was insinuating. "Why is that?"

"Oh I didn't tell you I'm going out of town?"

"No, you didn't tell me that!" Okay I know these moves. This fool thinks he is slick. He knows good and well he ain't tell me anything. But apparently he thinks short changing me and telling me at the last minute would keep the peace. I kept a straight face. I kept my voice as clear as possible to not seem bothered. "Where are you going?"

"My boys and I are taking a trip to Anguilla."

"OH!" I turned on my heels and headed back into the kitchen. How was I supposed to react to him telling me about this exotic trip he was taking without me? Yeah him and his boys alright.

136

I could hear him talking loud so that I could hear way in the kitchen. "Yeah I'm going to be gone an entire week. A much needed vacation."

I walked back in with a bottle of water in my hand. I wanted to throw the bottle at him. "Sounds like fun. Good for you."

Denim looked at me curiously and I swear I heard a hint of sarcasm in his voice. "I mean is that okay with you?" And if it wasn't then what? Your ass is still going to go.

"Is that a trick question or do you actually expect a response?"

"I mean I guess not huh?"

"You're a grown man D, if that's what you need to relax, go right ahead and enjoy. Movie time." I cut him off before he was able to say anything else and I was certain he wanted to change the subject anyway. I was beginning to know this man like the back of my hand. It didn't matter what I felt anyway because at the end of the day our relationship wasn't one anyway. What the hell were we doing then?

€€€

Diamond plopped across my bed as Nicole took a seat in my chaise and they both studied me. I wasn't trying to look either one of them in the eyes.

"What are you bitches looking at geesh?"

"So let me recap, that negro is going to Anguilla and he didn't invite you?" Diamond challenged me. We were all getting ready for the Essence Magazine mixer when I brought up the conversation I had with Denim yesterday.

Nicole added, "And you said nothing?"

I defended myself and yelled, "What was I supposed to say, don't go or take me with you?"

They both said in unison, "Yes!"

Diamond added, "That's your man so why the hell not?"

"He's not my man."

THE ███ I Didn't Say

Nicole dropped her head in her hand and blew out hot air. "Y'all two are giving me a headache. Y'all say y'all love each other. Talk every damn day all day long but y'all ain't together? Where they do this bullshit at?"

"Exactly," I said placing on a tight fitted red dress.

"Who came up with this arrangement? Him?" Nicole asked.

"No, we both did. In the very beginning we agreed we would just be. Enjoy each other."

"Hell and are you still enjoying him?" Diamond asked.

I walked into my room and sat down on the edge of my bed. "I can't come to him and change my mind and be like I only want you."

"Why the hell not? Enlighten Diamond and I because we are totally confused."

"How would you feel if someone changed up on you? Tell you the complete opposite of what you two agreed on?"

Diamond said, "I get that and all but you two love each other so what's so bad about telling him you want more? Afraid he won't say the same in return?"

Nicole added, "You should say it for yourself baby girl, not for him. If he is what you want go after it."

I studied my sisters for what seemed like hours. They had valid points but I also had valid points. "I don't know."

"How will you know if you don't say anything girl? Be fearless. Go get your man shit. Or someone else will."

"I don't want to lock him down just so nobody else will have him. I want him because he completes me. I love him."

My sisters both folded their arms and scolded me. I looked at them innocently until I realized the words that had just left my mouth.

"He completes me," I repeated. I pulled out my cell phone and searched Denim's number. Selecting messenger I drafted a message.

"What are you texting him?" Nicole asked studying me.

"Just what I said to you guys."

It's not that I need anyone to complete me. It's that I need someone to accept me completely. I love you.

Diamond snatched my phone and yelled, "Trick this is not what you told us. Tell that man you want him and call it a day."

I slipped into my shoes and said, "One day I will just not today. Let's go."

***

I walked into the Baldwin Hall with Nicole and Diamond. I had seen many of the Atlanta socialites here at plenty of events before. I had hugged and greeted a few actors and reality stars before taking up shop at a table near the far right of the room. Since Nicole was an honoree, she had to go and network with the people.

"I am so proud of our baby girl," Diamond said, taking a sip of her wine.

I agreed with her as I felt the buzzing of my phone. I looked at the unread messages and saw one from Claire. She was here and was looking to see where we seated. I gave her the directions and began to look for her off in the distance.

I saw an unread message from Denim that read: I love you too. See you in a bit.

"Ugh what the hell are you over there cheesing at? Please don't say Denim. I am tired of you always talking about him. What happened to the others?"

"Like who?"

"Well Kelvin for one."

I waved Diamond off. "Oh he's around and so are the others."

She shook head and laughed, "That's my bitch. I know you ain't ready to settle down like you are portraying."

I noticed Claire walking over and my smiled spread but it was erased with confusion as I stared at her date. Diamond laughed and said, "Looks like your girl Claire is taking pointers from you." I gave Diamond the evil eye and immediately tried to correct my face and my demeanor. Claire was here with Lewis.

THE ████ I Didn't Say

"Hey ladies!" I eyed her and gave her a head to toe assessment and I did the same to Lewis.

"Well you two look nice tonight." I wasn't lying. They looked good together. They even had matching glows. Looking at them made me wish that they would just commit to each other. They would be good together. "What's going on with you two?" I wanted to say to Claire how bold she was to walk in here without her husband on her arm.

"I'm good. How are you babe?" Claire leaned in and kissed my cheek. I did the same to Lewis as we all took a seat.

"So who is this?" Diamond asked. I eyed her. The girl held no filter. She always went straight in.

"Oh I am sorry Diamond, girl this is my friend Lewis. Lewis this is Diamond, Janet's big sister. They all moved him from Texas a few years ago."

Lewis shook Diamond's hand and greeted her. "This is a nice event. So which one of you is being honored?"

I answered, "Our baby sister. She's walking around networking and such. Did you guys get drinks? I'll wave a server over."

As I stood up and got a server's attention I noticed Denim in the crowd. He was with Dalvin. I told everyone I would be right back as I made my way over to them. "Hey handsome."

Hearing my voice, Denim turned and extended his arms for me to walk into his embrace. I hurriedly did because he was looking extra scrumptious tonight. "Hmmm you smell good babe. You look good too."

I was undressing him with my eyes. I loved how his tall dark appearance dominated my eyesight. He smiled and studied me. "Babe really?" He knew I was thinking about him the worst way at this moment. I couldn't help it. He was just so damn sexy.

"I'm sorry," I said staring at his bottom lip.

He laughed and kissed me. "So where are we sitting?"

I pointed in the direction of my table and told him to come along. I said hello and hugged Dalvin when I spotted Nicole.

"Oh wait there's Nicole you guys can speak to her while she has a moment." I waved her over.

"Hey Big D and Baby D." Nicole joked addressing Denim and Dalvin hinting that Dalvin was the Baby D.

"Hey baby girl, congrats on everything." Denim hugged Nicole as did Dalvin.

"Thanks brother-in-law. This night is magical you know."

Nicole went on and on about all the people she was missing. I couldn't help but notice that Denim didn't laugh or joke this time when Nicole called him brother-in-law. She had several times before it seemed to be the butt end of a joke but not this time. This time he just went with it.

"You look nice tonight too," Dalvin added. I couldn't help but see the interest in his eyes as I cleared my throat.

"Like really Dalvin."

He turned and looked at me innocently. "What?" He smirked.

"Get your eyes off of my baby sister. It's not going down."

"Dang what a way to call me out. I was just complimenting the woman."

"Baby let them live." Denim waved them off and pushed me the opposite direction towards our table.

"I don't want that negro talking to Nicole. He's a hoe just like…" My words trailed off as I almost stumbled over my own two feet as Denim pushed me backwards. He looked down to me and raised his eyebrow.

I stared at him he stared at me. "A hoe like who? Me?"

Shoot he had me there. Yep I was insinuating him, but we were in a so-called relationship and we were in a good place right now. Did I want to insult him? No. Did I want to call him out on his crap at this very moment? No. So I smiled slightly and said, "No, like most men I know."

"Yeah whatever." Denim let the subject slide, thankfully. We both knew who I was talking about anyway. Denim was a hoe. Even I wasn't enough for him to want to change.

THE 🖤 I Didn't Say

We took our seats at our table and we all got wrapped into a causal conversation. Dalvin and Nicole had taken on a night of their own and were dancing on the dance floor enjoying the night.

Denim leaned over and whispered in my ear, "You look beautiful babe." I looked over to him and smiled.

We just sat there and smiled at each other, our eyes having yet another conversation. My eyes dropped to his lips and I studied them. I loved his lips. They aligned with the darkness of his skin but the soul of his lips were a pretty pink, large, full, and soft.. A moaned escaped my mouth before I could catch it. Of course Diamond caught it and blurted out, "Damn sis looks like you want to rape Denim right here at the table."

Everyone laughed.

I laughed it off and said, "Perhaps I do. Would you all watch?" My voice was serious and stern. Lewis had a curious eye. Diamond's mouth dropped in what seemed like excitement, Claire eyed me with confusion, and Denim well he leaned back in his seat with a cocky glare. I knew he would like the sound of that.

"Bitch you are something else," Diamond laughed. "Gone head with your bad self."

"No, please stop." Claire said nearly clenching her teeth. I waved her off and laughed.

"Denim how does that sound to you?"

He licked his lips and leaned into my space. "Sounds perfect baby girl. Sounds damn good to me."

He passionately kissed my lips and I felt the initial effect of his touch shoot straight to my pearl. Instantly becoming engorged I squirmed in my seat to get more conformable but I could feel the initial wetness of my desire trace my inner lips there.

"How is she feeling?" He eyed my inner thighs and smiled.

"Painful. She needs a release," I whispered back.

We made sure to keep our conversation quiet but I was now looking for an outlet. Perhaps the restroom would do. A back closet room, an empty banquet hall; anything would do at this moment. I bit my bottom lip and began to look around.

142

"I know this place. There are some offices on the second floor. One is bound to be unlocked." Denim whispered in my ear while slipping his tongue out in between his whispers and tracing my ear lobe with the tip of his tongue.

I nodded my head okay as he grabbed my hand pulling me away from the table. We marched towards the elevators and pressed up. "Don't look obvious babe. Stay calm. I got you." He sealed his speech with a kiss as we stepped on the elevator and pressed the number two.

***

We lucked up with door number five. The copy room. I had never done something so spontaneous before. I felt the evidence of my excitement completely saturate my panties. Denim gripped my hand tightly and pulled me inside. "Lock the door," I whispered.

"Nah it's more fun if we leave it unlocked."

I felt the initial invasion of his hands as they trailed up my thigh hiking up my dress in the process. I felt like I heard the intro of one of R. Kelly's baby making songs.

I arched my back placing my ass on top of an empty table spreading my legs eagle style. "Take them off," I whispered.

Denim knelt down on his knees and with his teeth he pulled at my black lace thong panties and began to peel them away from my flesh. I rocked my body to the rhythm of his mouth from side to side like an erotic ocean. If the room was absolutely silent you could probably hear the drips of my love escape from my wetness onto the floor. One drip at a time I grew hotter and impatient.

Denim allowed his top lip to flick my pearl as he continued before he moved downward pulling my thong down my legs. He moaned hungrily as my smell began to engulf the room's air. I smelled sweet. I took huge breaths as I felt the rise and fall of my chest. I could no longer see Denim but I could feel that he now had my thong free. I heard them drop to the floor.

He pushed me backwards without warning and I fell like a doll on top of the table. As if he was angry with me and needing to get me to act right he aggressively pushed my legs further apart. Further than even my gynecologist would ask for and in one drop he lowered his face over my wetness and breathed in her smell. He growled. "Damn baby," he whispered.

With the flick of my pearl with the tip of his tongue I squirmed nearly in convulsions. He did it repeatedly, licking and sucking dipping his tongue inside of me and drawing back my ink. With his tongue and my juices he wrote me the most intimate message, "I breathe you!"

I felt the initial explosion of my orgasm rise to an unbearable level. I gripped my own legs cuffing them around my arms to embrace the impact and just as I was getting ready to explode Denim stood up, dropped his pants in a split second, and entered me. I scream out.

You could hear the slapping our flesh against one another as we became one. The rise and fall of our bodies were entwined with one another and in this moment I had everything I had ever wanted. Him inside of me.

Claire

It was the next morning. I turned over on my side and looked at the clock. Sunday mornings were usually my time to run or catch up on some things that needed to be done around the house.

"Morning."

I turned over as if there was a stranger in my house and tried to focus my eyes as the sun's brightness was making it hard to see. I looked in the doorway of my bedroom and see Evan standing there. "Hey!" I replied back.

"What's on your agenda today?"

"Nothing special," I said rising up and sitting on the side of my bed.

"Want to go into the city for lunch today. I don't have to go into the lot today. I turned it over to my manager. He'll control everything for me today."

He walked in and sat beside me on the bed. I subconsciously scooted the opposite direction and when I noticed my reaction, I eyed him to see if he did too.

He did. It was written all over his face.

"Babe!"

I sulked, becoming maybe two inches smaller as I grew weary of his tone. I just didn't want to be bothered right now. Not ever actually. "Yeah?" My response was dry. It held no interest. I actually wasn't interested in whatever it is that he wanted to talk about. We had nothing to talk about. I was over it. I was over him. Damn was I?

THE I Didn't Say

"I know I was wrong for what I did. I am sorry. How many times must I say that?"

"Are you speaking of the time when you actually molested your wife in her own home? Is that what you are talking about? Because if not, maybe it's for the extracurricular activities we both know you are involved in." My voice was so calm that I even scared myself.

He looked at me stunned at my bluntness. I didn't want to be bothered and I knew that cutting straight to what it was he was hesitating to say would end this conversation. I gave a soft chuckle before rising from where I sat and walked into my bathroom.

"I'm going for my run."

It was merely a couple minutes that had passed as I brushed my teeth. I heard Evan walk in behind me and stand in the doorway. "For a run huh?"

I talked through the toothbrush and paste in my mouth. "Yep, why what's up? You're all in my face this morning."

He dropped his head and ran his hands across his beard. "When did you get this smart ass mouth?" I shrugged my shoulders. "You didn't use to talk to me like this."

"I didn't use to have to share my husband either."

"What?"

I spit out the paste and splashed water across my face and then bolted it with a dry towel. I turned and leaned my body against the island. "What do you want damn spit it out already."

"I want to know what's going on with my wife."

I turned on my heels and marched into my walk in closet to grab my running gear. "Why what's up? Is your other chick busy? Did she drop you? I do not understand why you all of a sudden want to give me attention."

He fell silent before saying, "Is this why you brought someone to the Essence mixer with you last night?"

My back was to him and I was turned around grabbing my gear and thank God, the look on my face was shock. It wasn't even

146

twenty-four hours and he knew about last night. I place on my game face and simply said, "Nope!"

He laughed. Not that he was laughing at anything funny but it was more of I'm mad and annoyed kind of laugh. I turned and faced him and raised an eyebrow practically challenging him to say something else. "You have changed."

"Have I now?"

He face grew serious, he tone was now dark, and his demeanor was straight upward as he stared at me. "Are you fucking him? Something you haven't done with me in weeks."

"Maybe that's because you treated me like I was a whore on the streets. And no I am not."

He took a step towards me when I yelled out, "Come at me and try to fight me like I am a man. I promise you I will fight you back with all my might just like a man. I am not scared of you Evan."

"Oh you're not? Oh yeah you're big and bad now huh?"

I threw up my hands in annoyance, "What else is it? I said I am not fucking him. Yeah we went out last night. I mean; we went out many nights. You wouldn't know anyway because you're always with your whores."

He didn't blink. I shook my head in disgust. I had accused this man of cheating on me in more times in the last five minutes then the life of our relationship and he never flinched. He never denied it either. That just told me everything I needed to know. I never had real proof that was he doing me wrong, I just had a feeling that he always was.

"Fly on your own then lady. Fly on your own out of my house."

I looked at him and laughed, "You're playing that game?"

"I'm playing that game." He reassured me with a cocky stare.

"This game seems so easy for you to play too huh? Don't think I am that same ass weak Claire who just turns a blind eye to your bullshit. That isn't the case anymore. You want me gone, you will pay up."

THE I Didn't Say

He places his hands in his pockets and laughs, "Is that so?"

"I'll be gone. Today." I gave him the same smirk he was giving me. "As soon as you step out of my way."

Something in me told me to play this one safe and so I opted out of acting like a hard ass while I stood in a closed in closet with no weapon or phone. The way he was looking at me I didn't know what he was capable of doing.

He took a couple steps backwards but only allowing enough space for me to have to squeeze my way through. I could feel my heart began to rise with fear and anxiety. I didn't want to show weakness either. That would give him more power to taunt me.

I took a few steps towards him as I felt that suddenly the oxygen in this room became nonexistent. Inch by inch as I move towards him he stood his ground barely moving a muscle or blinking. It was as if he dared me to make any sudden moves. Oh I wasn't planning on it. I knew when the odds were against me and this man that stood before me suddenly looked like a stranger. And I didn't know what strangers were capable of.

I with my running shoes in my left hand I moved passed him swiftly eying the open door to my bedroom as the gateway to freedom. As I passed him I felt my arm brush across his chest and I cringed with fear. I don't know why I was afraid but something told me to be. I kept my face blank. I didn't want him to read into what my mind was thinking.

When I thought I was safely by him and I couldn't see him in my view I felt a sudden rush up behind me. I jerked forward without looking back and yelled out, "Get away from me!"

I could hear the pacing of Evan's feet as I ran through my bedroom. With only the silk pajamas I had slumbered in, I made the judgment to rush out of my house. I was a runner, Evan was not. I thought that if I ran as fast as I could. If I didn't look back and just focused on the exit strategy that I would be okay. That's it; no matter if you feel he's right behind you don't look back.

I made it out my bedroom. I eyed the flight of stairs.

I rushed towards them leaping over two steps at a time and but sometimes missing and having to do one at a time. I stumbled on the sixth step and heard him close in on me. This was how we were going to end, my running out of my own house?

This wasn't always us. I used to be in love.

€€€

I lay on my left side and watched him and his brother bring in box after box into our new home. It was beautiful. It was everything I had ever imagined. The room had a yellowish peach look to it I made a decision to paint it cherry blossom red in that moment. "This color has to go right babe?"

"You better be glad you over there carrying my seed or I would be putting your butt to work," Evan laughed out. I blew him a kiss and rubbed my belly.

"I'm lifting with you in spirit." I stuck my tongue out as we laughed it off.

I heard Janet waltz in breathing extra heavy as if she had just ran a marathon. "Lookahere I didn't sign up to perform all of this domesticated work now. Claire where do you want this ugly ass lamp."

Janet stood in my doorway completely exhausted. I gave her encouraging praises but couldn't hide my mockery of a smile. "I will fight a pregnant woman now," she teased.

"That's my late grandfather's lamp Janet. Don't call it ugly," I whined, pretending to be a baby.

"Evan do you see your wife milking this situation for all its worth. I can't stand her." Janet laughed and placed the lamp on my dresser. "Here I'm going to leave this treasured lamp here," she said sarcastically.

"I swear I can't stand her either," he laughed.

As Janet turned on her heels I called out, "Best friend can you please make me a turkey sandwich. Your nephew is hungry." Janet didn't bother to turn around she threw up her middle finger as I called out, "I love you too."

THE ![word] I Didn't Say

I eyed Evan prepping to walk back outside to the moving truck and smiled. "Thank you for giving me this life babe. I love you."

He smiled and walked over to me. He leaned down he kissed the tip of my nose and said, "I love you too baby." He eyed my belly and rubbed it gently, "I love you too little man. Alright babe, I got to go get the rest of your things."

I smiled brightly, "I'm excited."

"I know babe. Me too, me too."

€€€

I eyed the last two steps and attempted to leap to the last one and slipped, falling on my right side. I rolled over to make it easier for me to get back up when I noticed Evan racing down the steps. My heart raced so quick that the tightening of my chest make me feel thirty pounds heavier.

"Stop!" I screamed out hoping that my screams who scare him straight. His eyes were pierced with rage. His shoulders were bucked and his body was ready to charge. "It's me. It's me. Stop!" He was mere inches away from me as I was scooting backwards on my bottom.

"You think you can just leave Claire. You think you can just walk away that easily? Look what I built for you. I built a life for you here." He was screaming at the top of his lungs as his body towered over mine. He was towering over me so closely that our noses nearly touched.

"And you haven't been here!" I shot back. "You haven't been here since..." I voice trailed off. I didn't want to think about it. I didn't want to remember the agony and the pain of it all. The day I lost my child was the day I lost my husband too.

€€€

Close your eyes, count to five. Push. Over and over that's all I kept hearing. I rolled my eyes at the nurse who was encouraging me and then at Evan who was acting like I was a player on the court making the sweetest three pointer. "Calm your ass down and get out of my face," I huffed.

I was in pure agony. I pushed away from Evan as I felt the impact of another contraction. I screamed out, "Here's another one."

"Okay get ready to push," The doctor said again. It had thirty minutes now and I was all out of gas. I felt I was going to die soon from the mere fact that I couldn't find any more strength to push.

I looked at Evan who was eyeing the doctor and the nurse weirdly. Another nurse walked over towards them as they stared at the monitors. Something wasn't right and it was written all over his face. My current pain was not overshadowed by my fear and confusion.

"What is it?"

The doctor stood up quickly and attempted to talk to me calmly. "We're going to have to take you in surgery the baby is in distress."

"What?" we asked in unison.

They began to move around the room the room so quickly without warning that my eyes paced back and forth to get an understanding of what was going on around me. I could hear Evan asking question after question nearly shouting at the nurses when I heard one of them say, "Sir we don't have time to just discuss what needs to be done. We are taking her up to OR 5."

I was shuffled out of the room and rushed down the hall. They spoke to me so fast I could barely keep up with what they were telling me and I went into panic. I could no longer see Evan any more. It was just me.

The OR room was in panic mode as I noticed so many people moving around, yelling orders, and prepping for what would be my child's birth. I was lifted out of the bed I was once on and placed on flat bedding, more like a table. The worst was yet to come and it came after my child was born.

€€€

THE ▓▓▓ I Didn't Say

"Since when Claire, huh tell me?"

My eyes were blot shot red from the amount of tears and fear that filled them. I stared this man in the eyes. That is what scared me the most. I could recognize him by his eyes, his smile, his voice and none of that was familiar right now. He was so dark that he could have been dead.

"It happened okay. We lost him alright. Nothing we could do to change it. And you stopped trying after he died. You stopped loving me and I just accepted it."

Evan reached out and grabbed me by my top and yanked me upward. I screamed out for him to let me loose.

"You don't talk about him in this house!"

He threw me down on the wooden floor from where he first pulled at me. I screamed out as the collision shot jolts of pain through my ass and lower back.

"Get the hell away from me!" I screamed again.

"So now you want to fuck around on me?"

Evan marched over to me as I kicked backwards closer to the front door. I could feel the heaviness on my chest as panic began to smother me. I felt as if I weren't breathing. In that moment I felt that my life was not my own. I felt Evan held all the cards and held my fate in his hands and I didn't like feeling powerless.

I screamed at the top of my lungs as he reached down and aggressively covered my mouth. He gripped the back of my head and resembled just knew that he was going to snap my neck. My eyes grew wide with fear as I squirmed and kicked attempting to free myself. This is it. This is how I am going to die.

Janet

I stared at my cell phone awaiting a text from Denim but I kept getting texts from all the others I could care less about. I grew annoyed with the waiting but of course I wasn't going to text him. I found myself doing that often. I never wanted to catch him in the act with someone else or call and he couldn't pick up because he was with one of his women.

It bothered me that I didn't feel free enough to just be. I had to think and analyze everything. Shit shouldn't be this hard when you love someone. I blew out hot air and rose up from my bed. I opened all the windows in my bedroom and stared into the sky's dreamy blue. To get lost in Mother Nature is a blessing.

I needed an escape right now. I needed some companionship right now but I didn't want to be bothered with anyone but Denim. I kept thinking of the trip he was taking to Anguilla. Dalvin slipped up and mentioned a few people that were going and Lena was one. Why wouldn't he take me with him? Why didn't he offer it? It's not like I can just invite myself.

Sometimes I felt that Denim did love me but he didn't love me enough for me to be a daily factor in his life. Often times I felt I filled a position his other women didn't. I was the one who got the talks, the stories of his past dreams and aspirations, I got the sweeter side of him, and he needed me to be that go to girl.

But I needed him to be that man for me too. I needed to feel like I held some stake in his life. But I was beginning to think that I actually didn't. I mean who were his sisters, his mom, his dad, and his friends outside of Dalvin I had never been introduced to anyone. Hell, I didn't even know anyone's name.

THE ~~████~~ I Didn't Say

I grew frustrated as I began to run through the facts in my head. I wasn't as close to Denim as I thought and I wanted more. I wanted more of him and I wanted it more often.

I was pulled out of my thoughts when I heard the sudden rings of my phone. I threw myself across my bed and looked at the caller ID. I pressed talk and sang out, "Hey hey hey!"

"Hey baby girl what are you up to?" Diamond's voice was high pitched and cheery.

"Nothing just lounging. Gonna go into the office later tonight. Gonna do some late night working today. What are you doing?"

"I called to give you some juice. So apparently your baby sis and Dalvin have been getting kind of close."

I raised an eyebrow. "Kind of close how? Oh boy I do not need them two to be starting up to make it uncomfortable for everyone else."

Diamond laughed, "I told Nicole you would say that same exact thing."

"Whatever, so have they had sex?"

"Not that I know of but she said they went out since meeting at the Essence event last night."

"Damn already, they must really like each other."

"Yeah he mentioned he was going out of the country to her and that your boy was going too."

I immediately grew annoyed and blew out air as my eyes rolls around in my head. "What now Diamond?"

"Whaaa hey I didn't say anything, yet!"

"Go on say what you got to say so we can get this conversation over."

"Ewe why all of a sudden your ass got an attitude with me? Looks like it needs to be geared towards Denim. Sooooo are you made that he plans to go out of the country for a week without his woman?"

"First of all I am not his woman and he can do whatever he wants."

"How does that sound to you Janet, seriously? I am your sister you can be honest with me okay. Stop the tough girl act."

I grew quiet. I don't know why I felt less of a woman to reveal my insecurities. Maybe it was because I wasn't naturally an insecure woman. But Denim did that to me. He made me feel like I wasn't protected. He made me feel like I loved an unstable connection. Our connection was nothing like I had ever experienced but it was also incomplete. It was incomplete simply because I didn't truly hold a place in his life. He spoke, he said it often, but his words were beginning to bounce off of my heart like I had on a bullet proof vest.

"I'm not happy."

"Okay here is a start. I am listening baby girl just talk to me."

"Ever since Desmond broke my heart you have seen me in action. I treat guys as if they were replaceable, having unattached sex, and I limited my communication with them outside the bedroom. No one gets close. That's the vow I took on."

"True!" Diamond edged on.

"But after meeting him…his broken heart matched my broken heart. We connected, but at the same time, we were both stuck in our ways. We said we wanted no strings, but we did every opposite thing that wouldn't involve strings. We fell in love Diamond."

"I know baby girl."

"How can I tell this man that I changed my mind and that I want more?"

"You just say it Janet, what else do you have to lose?"

"Him!"

Diamond raised her voice slightly, "If that man walks away because the woman he says he loves tells him that she loves him I am done with that negro. He can get hit by a bus. Who does this stupid shit? You and he are way too difficult. Y'all truly get on my nerves."

"He's the difficult one!" I shot back.

"Oh really; well if that is true why are telling me this and not him?"

I opened my mouth to speak but she had a good question. I hated when she was right. "Alright big sis. I'll do it tonight. Promise."

"Don't promise me anything baby girl, do it for you okay."

"Okay!"

"I love you!"

"I love you too Diamond."

Click.

€€€

I walked into my office to see if Claire was pounding away at her keyboard but she was missing. We both rarely worked on a Sunday that wasn't out of the ordinary. But I needed to work. Denim would be busy working for the next few days and I planned to meet him later to talk. Although he didn't know we needed to talk.

I sat down behind my desk and pressed play on my iPod and soon the sounds of Aaron Hall filled the air. I began to perform my usual ritual checking my emails first. I heard the buzzing sound of my cell phone as I had it on silent and went to reach for it. I noticed it was Denim and my heart skipped.

It was often that I received a text or a call and saw his name and my entire body felt light. I could float into the Earth's atmosphere with the emotions that ran through my body with just the thought of him. I shook my head and pretended to not be as affected by his call as I answered with a routine hello. "Hey you!"

"Hmmm hey baby what are you doing?" His deep sultry voice made me squirm in my seat. This man made me want to have sex on demand.

"I am at my office working. What are you doing?"

"At the studio. One of my other producers just took over a session. I am going to be busy all day. I wanted to squeeze in some Janet time. Is that okay with you?"

"Oh some Janet time huh?"

"Yeah I need to feel you right now."

"I need to feel you too. You wanna meet up or do you want to come here?"

"I'll be there in thirty minutes."

"Okay, see you then."

Denim

The silence engulfed me as I walked onto Janet's floor. I suddenly could only hear the beating of my heart and the rapid pace of my breaths. Sometimes seeing her felt like it was for the first time. Crazy I know, but she just did that for me. It would be moments where I could just stare at her and admire her beauty. She didn't have to speak or even look a certain way. She was naturally beautiful to me.

I bypassed the closed doors to her adjoining offices and made my way to her. "Babe are you safe in here by yourself?" I asked as I neared and could hear her on her computer.

"Hey you. Security is here, plus I have my stun gun." She pulled out her weapon, it was pink and small and I laughed.

"Okay yeah that will scare someone off." I leaned down and kissed her routinely on her lips.

"Hmm one more please." She begged as I fulfilled her request.

"So what are you doing today?" I took a seat across from her as she sat at her desk and studied her.

"One sec babe let me finish this email and then I am all ears."

I waved her off and told her that it was fine. I wasn't a jealous man by far. I enjoyed the fact that Janet was passionate about her work

"You know every time you are focused in on something that dimple appears right in the middle of your forehead."

Halfway listening, Janet looked at me with a confused expression, placing her hand on her forehead. "Excuse me?"

"Nah babe don't cover it. I love it." I leaned over her desk removing her hand and kissed her temple. "It's cute," I teased.

"Hahahaha Mr. Igotjokes. Okay I'm done," she said, shutting off her computer. "I wanted to talk to you anyway."

I patted my lap. "Come on and sit in Daddy's lap. Tell me all about it."

"Stop teasing me D." She laughed and sat down in my lap wrapping her right arm around my neck as the other lay in her lap.

"So when you say we need to talk does that mean you actually want to talk?" I asked.

She stared at me blankly. "I do have to say this. It's kind of eating at me."

I didn't want my disinterest to show on my face simply because there would be another talk about my reaction and this and that. But I was willing to put up with whatever Janet was about to say simply because it was her. I cared about her more than anyone I had ever cared for in my life. I loved her, but there were limits to my love. Some I would rather not her know but hey, if she wanted to talk, let's talk.

"You're leaving in a couple days and I feel that we're in such a good place that I don't want it interrupted you know."

"Okay," I said, not knowing where this was headed.

"I love you but sometimes I feel that you are careless with my feelings."

I stopped her in midsentence. "Babe when we started we said no strings, no titles, none of that and I feel this conversation is about to lead to something that will contradict that."

"I know what we said D, but honestly we have been doing so much. We have been doing everything that says that we are more than just friends."

"True. I understand that but—"

"But what?"

I took a deep breath and patted her legs to signal for her to hop out of my lap. "Janet. I love you yes, and I am trying, trust me on that. I have opened up to you. You have opened up to me and we're good right?"

THE ![symbol] I Didn't Say

Silence.

I studied her waiting for a response. "We're good right?"

"Why would you go on a trip without me if we're so good?" She shot back at me.

"What?" I lowered my head and dropped it in my hands in an effort to not get frustrated. "Babe I booked that trip in the beginning of us. We weren't who we are now and besides I can use the vacation from everything."

"From me?" She shot out again.

I picked up on her ever changing mood and shook my head. She was challenging me. I hadn't had these types of conversations before because no one ever got close enough for me to even bother with this. I didn't want Janet to become one of those things I regretted. I mean, if she just stopped talking and questioning everything we would be fine. Just let us be.

It may sound selfish. But at least I can admit my being selfish and just go with it. At this point I didn't care if Janet wanted me to go or not because I was going.

"I don't need a break from you babe, it's just I need a break from this environment. You know I love you." I would be lying if I said I didn't sometimes say I love you to soften her up. Most women would love for a man to just say those three words so I said it often especially when we were in a rough space.

"Yep I know." She dryly responded hopping up out of my lap. "Listen I have some work to complete, perhaps we can meet up later. I mean, if you aren't busy." Janet didn't even look my way as she found herself back behind her desk.

I noticed the straightening of her back and the arch in her eyebrows. Her shield. I didn't want that. But I wanted my freedom too so I ignored the signs of her shutting down on me and walked over to her and kissed her forehead.

"I'll call you later on babe." She didn't respond as I walked out of her office. I switched gears and text Dalvin to meet me for dinner. I still had an hour of spare time and instead of spending it in the studio or with a moody Janet I would spend it with my best friend.

€€€

"What up!" I gave Dalvin a one hand shake before sitting down at the bar to order drinks.

"I just want a beer and some wings," Dalvin said glancing over the menu.

"So what's up on your floor? Tell me about the Rock Nation campaign."

"Oh shit, I forgot to tell you man, after we come back from Anguilla the marketing director at Rock Nation wants to meet up about a Spring campaign. I think they are coming out with a new product they want us to help launch."

"Oh word? Sounds like a plan to me. Shit, I need to get more involved in work anyway. I swear this love shit is a distraction."

"Something up with you and Janet?"

I took a swallow of my beer and nodded my head yes. "She's asking a lot of questions. Wanting to go on the trip now."

"I thought telling her last minute would ease the transition but damn bro you know you got to put a lid on that. You know I'm your boy and all but you got yourself in a sticky situation if she knew who was going on that trip instead of her."

"Don't remind me."

"Level with me man, why not Janet?"

I studied Dalvin's questions locking my eyes on my half empty beer and said, "Too much time can equal too much trouble. With that woman I'm practically thinking of marriage."

"And that's a bad thing because?"

"Dog, marriage! Nah not me."

"I get it D, trust me. I was married. But I don't regret it. I loved that woman. The only reason why we ain't together is because she wouldn't accept my dirt. It'll be a perfect world if she were to just look the other way you know."

"You feel me? I mean this no titles shit with her was working. I was getting the best of both worlds. Janet gets every aspect of me and I am comfortable with being open with her, but then I can leave and go do whatever whenever I want. Perfect situation right."

"Yep! Selfish but yep!"

"Dude I know I am selfish, that's clear, but I am also honest."

Dalvin laughed and waved me off, "Man I recognize how you are using that honesty. It's like your Superman cape. You can do all your dirt and make it okay as long as you're honest."

"Exactly!" We laughed.

"And when she gets tired of that and recognizes what you are doing then what?"

"What?"

"What then negro? You heard me!"

"That woman ain't going anywhere. People search a lifetime for the connection her and I have. She won't find anyone better than me."

"Oh but Nitrah did!"

"Is the beer making you act like a female, what the hell? Nitrah and I were long ago, that was different."

"How so, you ain't been with a woman that serious since Nitrah. Janet is the first and man I hate to say it, but I am only because I miss my wife and all these chicken heads that come our way ain't amount to what I lost. They all see us and want something. But my wife didn't want anything. Janet doesn't want anything."

"Yeah I know!"

"Level with me man. I'm your boy, you can talk to me."

"I don't—"

He cut me off and said, "Dude I already know what's up it ain't like you got to say it. But you are going to mess around and lose that girl. And for what, for random fucks?"

I opened my mouth to speak but decided to drink my beer instead. "You know what my break up with Nitrah did to me. You were there!"

He shook his head yes. "Dog I know, but is that an excuse to keep this woman at arm's length. Man we are heading into our forties soon. Why not try something different. We've lived this life. We've done what we wanted this entire time, and for once since Nitrah you found someone that matches you. Someone who gets you."

"Shit is easier said than done Dalvin."

"Love is easy my friend. It's us who make this so difficult when it doesn't have to be. If Janet is asking questions now what do you think she will do later?"

"True!" I said pondering what he was telling me.

"Why would you tell that woman you loved her if you weren't willing to love her."

"I am loving her." I defended myself.

He shook his head. "D I am only being hard on you right now because you're my best friend. We go back since grade school, I know you and you know me. What kind of friend would I be if I didn't speak my truth about what I thought? And truth is I think you're going to fuck this one up. And then what; wait another twenty years for someone to get you? Dude I need another drink." Dalvin signaled to the bar tender to get us two more beers.

"Janet knows when the time is right we will move forward."

"Does she?"

I studied him and then his question before saying, "I'll make sure she does once I return from my trip."

Claire

"Love…it kills your heart. It steals your soul."- Obengbia Leyony

Breathe steady. Keep your eyes closed. Don't let him see you in pain. You are stronger than most. You can survive the worst. Simply because you are Claire. You are one of a kind and there will never be another you. So now breathe easy baby girl. Don't let him see you cry. The tears for him aren't worth it. You can cry when you are alone. You can reveal you are weaker than some when you are by yourself. But not now Claire. Do not show weakness. Breathe baby girl. Breathe deep. Breathe as if your soul depended on your very next breath to stay alive. Choose life. Choose light. Choose to not care for him. Because you are Claire. You will be fine.

I opened my eyes, barely able to focus in on what I was seeing. I was still cradled on the floor of my living room. And once I realized that I was still breathing in this world the pain became evident. I was hurt. Hurt where?

I had fought many of fights in my life, but this one I lost. The blood on my clothes was evidence. I heard silence as I used my other senses to see if anyone was near. I heard nothing. Just the creeps and crackles of the house and my breathing. I'm breathing!

I felt the heat from my tears drizzle down my cheeks and over my nose as I realized that I was still breathing. I was alive! But I was stuck. I was afraid to move because I didn't know where he was.

Do not move baby girl. Wait just a few more moments. Be sure.

I think I held my breath for so long that I nearly passed out from lack of oxygen. I opened my eyes slightly again and saw the legs of my couches and tables, and the exotic rug Evan and I bought at a flea market last Spring. I saw the evidence of my marriage before me. The evidence that I shared a home with someone. It was all there in its materialistic form but it meant nothing. It all meant nothing. I didn't want it. I hadn't wanted it for a while.

I noticed the brightness of the sun beaming through the windows and it was evidence that it was now day. The morning had passed. How long had I been lying here? Okay enough waiting. I have to make a move. I can't stay on this floor forever. He could be here. He could be gone and then come back.

I noticed my back was facing the table my keys usually were on. I was mere inches away from the front door. If I could manage to move and get them and get out I will be okay.

I took slow steady breaths. I winced at the obvious pain in my stomach. Then I remembered the kicks.

"You want to leave me?" Kick to my right side. "You will have to leave crawling." Kick to my back. I jerked at the memory of each kick that Evan hit me with as if he were doing it all over again.

If I rise from here and manage to be okay I am going to kill that man. I used as much strength as I could but each time I thought about the pain it weakened me. I decided to give myself one hard push and fight through it. I attempted to open my left eye and it didn't. Either that or I was now blind.

I could barely hold my head up. I can't drive. I can barely move. I eyed the security system and zoomed in on the panic button. One last attempt I pushed upward using the wall as a ladder and pressed it. I screamed out in pain as I managed to hit the button. The alarm sounded off. I fell back on the floor and cried out in pain as I waited for someone to come help me.

THE 🏭 I Didn't Say

€€€

I felt someone's hand holding mine. "Is this the worst case scenario?" I mumbled.

"Hey lady you're awake."

My eyes searched the room. I noticed Janet, my sister, my mom, and Lewis. My eyes stayed on him. Janet's eyes followed where I was staring as she said, "I called him."

I nodded my head that it was okay.

"Where is that husband of yours?" My mom shouted.

"I imagined somewhere flying in the wind, Mama. He's the reason I am in this bed right now." The room grew silent. "Tell me what's going on." I eyed Janet.

"Three broken ribs baby girl."

"Your eye is swollen shut but its okay, bruised lip, your right shoulder is fractured too Claire," my sister added.

I felt myself crying again. Janet reached over and began to rub my head. "So Evan huh. I figured so which is why I didn't call. But Mama here did."

"I didn't know. How did you know?" Mama asked.

"We haven't been getting along lately Mama. You know that ever since we lost the baby. This was coming," I blurted out. I was tired of her being in denial. She knew that my marriage was on the rocks. Hell it was nonexistent.

I eyed Lewis again. "Guys can you give us a moment?"

Janet and my sis kissed my forehead before leaving out. Mama on the other hand needed extra encouragement to leave. "I'll go speak to the police. They have been waiting for you to wake up," Janet said before leaving out with Mama.

The look in his eyes hurt my heart. Crazy thing is I felt bad that he had to see me this way. But thankfully that was only the only pain I was feeling at this moment. Whatever pain meds they had me on was working.

"I'm going to kill him," Lewis said just above a whisper.

I hadn't felt this close to anyone since Evan…. I mean the time when we were in love.

166

"I'm here. I'll be fine."

"Look...I'm sorry." Lewis came over and grabbed my hand and kissed my forehead.

"Don't apologize for this." I felt myself began to drift off as I attempted to speak again. "This medicine is going to have me out in a minute. I am glad you are here Lewis."

"I'll be right here until you go home too Claire. You can come to my home."

"Your home?" I challenged. He shushed me and told me not to think about it. I decided to keep quiet. I couldn't have this conversation right now anyway.

I closed my eyes and for the first time in a long time I felt at peace. With Lewis beside my bed it was more than I could ask for right now.

Janet

I needed a drink. A hard one. I signaled for the server to bring the drink menu. I had gathered my girls out tonight. I needed to release my stress. I needed to just be surrounded around my friends and my sisters. I began to sway to the music of Stacey Barthe when Diamond asked me, "So how is she?"

"Where is that sorry ass Evan anyway? You know I told y'all I didn't like his ass after they lost the baby," Nicole added.

I replied, "She's doing good actually and Evan hasn't showed up yet. But they are talking heavy charges."

"Good, he almost killed that girl," Tanya added.

"I just needed to get out you know? Not to act as if nothing happened but just to have a moment," I whined.

"Oh we understand," they all said in unison.

"So who's treating?" Jessica blurted. "I don't get paid until this weekend."

I waved her off, "I got you girl." Then I eyed Nicole. "So word is you are getting close to Dalvin."

Nicole blushed and looked away from the table. "He's cool that's all."

"Yeah yeah yeah this chick be texting that negro all day," Diamond added. "Y'all need to be more free like me. Bump all that falling in love crap."

"You say that now because your ass ain't in love," Tanya shot back.

"I mean I am not in love. But I am in strong like. He's nice. I like him," Nicole added, smiling from ear to ear.

I rolled my eyes and laughed. "Ugh you get on my nerves. Be careful he's best friends with the beast," I joked.

Diamond laughed, "Oh so now Denim is the beast and what are you beauty?"

I pondered her joke and laughed, "Well yes actually I am Ms. Smart Mouth."

"Oh Lord and the mood changes again," Diamond continued. I waved her off.

"Like really chick, I'm going to need you to stop with the jabs okay. I mean I love Denim but that man is selfish and unmovable. I can't stand him."

"You love him girl we know," Nicole added.

I rolled my eyes. "Ugh let me order some food."

Everyone laughed at my expense. "Girl if he ain't giving you what you want just drop his ass. You'll find more. What happened to Kelvin anyway?" Jessica asked.

"He's around. We hit each other up once we're bored with whomever we are dealing with."

"I see, like your safety net?" Nicole asked.

"Hell no girl, Kelvin is her side piece."

"Wait women have side pieces?" Tanya asked. The table grew silent as we all stared at her dumbfounded. "What I didn't know?"

"Girl please. A woman can have a side piece, cuddle buddy, that special someone you ain't committed to," I answered as Diamond eyed me, "and the one who lays down the pipe and goes on his merry way. Hmmm I loves that type."

Diamond laughed out.

"You sound like a man," Jessica judged.

"Girl I learned all my shenanigans from Diamond. That's why I had Paul Mr. Head Hunter."

"Ooo where is Paul?" Nicole asked.

"The hell if I know. It's been weeks since I have heard from him. I guess his time is done in my bed. I'll find a new one now worries," I assured everyone.

"You are tripping," Diamond shot out.

I rolled my eyes and forcibly threw my head into her line of sight. "What is it now Diamond damn."

"Oh no Miss Ihaveabackbone. Don't get all crunk on me now. I'm just listening to you talk about finding another head hunter verses fighting for your man."

I took a huge gulp of my drink and plopped back down in my seat. "You can't fight for a man who doesn't want to be kept."

"True!" Jessica agreed.

"Let's change the subject. Let's take a shot for our girl Claire." I announced. I signaled for the server to give us shots all around the table and once they did we raised our glasses for our girl and in one gulp gave her an honor.

"Okay now I am ready for some food." We all laughed as we continued to enjoy each other's company.

€€€

It was a couple of days before Denim was set to leave. I didn't want to be a Debbie Downer before he left. Besides the last thing I wanted to do was be on his bad side when he was going to be gone doing God knows what to God knows who.

Ask me how was I able to function knowing that the man I loved was going to be gone at some exotic hotel in a foreign country with another woman? Hell, I was still trying to figure it out myself. The main thing that didn't force me to hurt was the fact that we held no titles. But I also knew that we held no titles because it gave him freedom to do whatever. Me too. But my agenda was changing. I didn't want anyone else.

He had the best of both worlds and I ended up only craving his world. But did what I want even matter? Would it even make a difference if I asked him? Would asking him piss him off? I was tired of the mental tug of war.

I needed to spend time with him and make it nice and sweet . I bought his favorite cheesecake and cooked us some homemade chicken parmesan. I bought a bottle of the best red wine and placed it in my freezer and placed mango-scented candles on the table.

170

After I was satisfied with how everything was set up I took to my phone and text him.

Babe, are you on your way?

I walked back into the kitchen to check on the Marie Calendar pie I had simmering in the oven as I waited on his response. After fifteen minutes later I finally got:

Baby I am stuck at the studio it may be a minute.

I stared at my phone for what seemed was until the dark ages were reappearing. I was stuck in place attempting not to feel some type of way about being blown off. Did he not understand that he was leaving soon? I attempted so hard to hold my anger in that I felt pain in my chest.

I brought my hand to my chest and focused on my breathing. This is some straight up bullshit.

"I can't believe I am acting this emotional over a man," I said to myself. But he's not just a man Janet; you love him. Stop fighting it and just show him that you want him.

I plopped down at my kitchen table and pondered over the conversation I was having in my head. I was afraid to make any moves in fear of pushing Denim away. But at the end of the day I was tired of punking out. I'll just tell him. I'll just tell him I want only him, I want to try to make this work.

I stood up from my seat fidgeting at just the thought of being that open and that honest. I had never been that vulnerable with anyone since Desmond. But today I felt I was strong enough to do it. I wanted to be fearless. I was tired of the wondering. Every time I thought of Denim I thought about all the possibilities. I finally wanted him to know how I felt.

€€€

I reached into my back seat and pulled out the Tupperware container of food I had packed for Denim and marched into the building he worked in.

I had noticed the remodeling that had been performed on the lobby. The accent rugs and black art that graced the walls gave it an art museum feel. I smiled noticing an original Tom Handle painting that hung near the elevators. He was a local painter I told Denim about a couple months ago.

Stepping onto the elevator I pressed for the second floor and waited for the doors to reopen. Stepping off, I could hear the sounds of hip hop music blaring through the air. I bounced my head to the beat liking what I was hearing. I wonder if that's a new song Denim is working on.

I didn't see anyone immediately but soon saw a few people passed me by or walked the hallways as I walked towards studio B, the one Denim used faithfully.

Finally there I placed all the Tupperware in my left hand and pressed it up against myself to hopes to not drop it as I placed my hand on the knob to turn it. I smiled brightly at just the thought of his expression once he saw me but I dared not to announce myself as I didn't want to interrupt a recording and throw them off.

I stepped in and saw a couple people seated on a couch towards the back and then I spotted Denim at the sound board focused on whatever it is that those board things did. When I smiled and opened my mouth to speak I was interrupted by a familiar voice. "Babe I found this in the breakroom."

My mouth drop, my eyes pierced zooming in on my target. I couldn't believe my eyes. "Jessica!" I announced.

At the sound of my voice Jessica turned and saw me standing in the doorway and became stuck in place. Her eyes shot from me to Denim then from Denim to me. Then he looked at me. He stood up so quickly my head had to readjust quickly to look up towards him. I slowly walked in a few more steps allowing the door to close behind me.

I hadn't blinked. I hadn't breathed. I hadn't uttered a word. It was written on everyone's face. We were all telling each other how we felt through our emotions. Jessica read, 'I'm busted'. Denim's read 'I'm busted and I'm about to get into some shit'. Mine read confusion.

"Babe hey!" Denim calmly spoke to me as if I was a crazy person about to hold the place hostage.

"Umm yeah explain!" Do not show weakness. Do not cry in front of these people. You are bolder than that. I readjusted my emotions and placed on my game face. I knew I would break down but I refused to give them the satisfaction of seeing me cry.

Jessica stood back and clasped her hands together refusing to make eye contact with me. I eyed her and called her out on it taking my attention from Denim to her. "So you're fucking him? You are bold enough to be with him and you can't even look me in the face." I sat down the Tupperware of food I had prepared and laughed. "This is some mess. Why even bother with negros like you." I was talking to myself but loud enough for Denim to hear.

"Babe I don't know what to say. I am sorry. I didn't want you to know about this."

"When Denim? When did you start sleeping with my friend?" I eyed him and dared him to look away. I was that close to dropping my keys and my purse and placing a beating on his ass.

"A few weeks ago."

I dropped my head and shook it in disbelief. "I could hurt you right now. I could beat the life out of you Jessica. For you to sit and smile in my face just yesterday. 'Leave him alone if he won't commit' you said. Oh it makes sense now why you want me to leave him alone huh?"

"It just kind of happened one night. I am sorry Janet."

"Is not serious babe, you know how I do. I mean you know we're not together," Denim said that line with so much confidence I wanted to slap two shades of black off of him.

"But my friend! You fuck my friend?" I screamed at the top of my lungs. I couldn't believe my ears. I never care. I never give a man a time of day to have a chance to win my heart and the very one I tell I love you tells me he can fuck my friends because we have no titles.

I was in the twilight zone. Where were his boundaries? Where was his respect for my feelings? When was enough enough?

THE ▓▓▓ I Didn't Say

I couldn't hide the pain at this moment. I could feel my eyes burning with anger and pain.

I pressed up against a nearby table and gripped my heart. It was so heavy. I felt my heart was beating in slow motion and that my blood was as thick as syrup that it was working overtime to get my blood flowing. I winced out in pain as Denim attempted to rush over towards me and ask if I were okay.

"Don't come near me," I screamed. "So this is how the game goes right?"

"What game babe? I have always been honest with you."

"You use honesty for bad D, can't you see that. It's like you tell me I ate the last piece of your favorite cake but don't be mad at me because I told you I ate it. The point is that you ate it. The point is that you are hurting me. That doesn't justify your actions. You're trying to make your actions okay. It's not okay!"

Denim leaned against his sound board and placed his hands in his pockets. "I…I never wanted to hurt you Janet."

I eyed him for what seemed like an eternity and it was starting to all make sense. "Denim you hurt me the day you decided to tell me you loved me but chose to not be different with me. You chose to not try to see if I was just enough for you. You never tried to make me and you work. You never attempted to see if I were enough."

Denim didn't speak. His eyes read that he understood everything that I was saying. But understanding it wasn't the point. I was facing the fact that he thought it was ok to cross that line with my friend. Where was my level of respect?

"How would you feel if I slept with Dalvin?"

Silence.

I waited. Still silence.

"How would you feel if I slept with Dalvin?" I asked again.

"I wouldn't like that." Denim confessed.

I dropped my hands to my side, "What's the point of saying I love you anyway if in the end I don't have you." I began to turn and eyed the food I made for him. "Well if you're hungry

Jessica and you can eat the food I took time to make for you." I didn't look at her again as I walked out. She wasn't worth talking to at this point.

I walked out and rushed towards the elevator. I was in my car in a matter of minutes speeding off into a much needed escape. The tears I cried made it hard to focus but I managed to breathe and drive and make it home. I closed my door, closed all my curtains and escaped the world for a minute. I needed nothing but my journal and so I went to bed and wrote.

Janet

Dear Janet,

Life can deal you many cards. The whole purpose of us being down here is to live life right. To do well with Life and then go to heaven. That is what we are taught and often times we challenge it. We challenge it in everything that we do.

I fell in love with a man who shared the same views on life as I did. The difference between him and I is I tend to want to control the outcome of life. It's weird huh because no one holds the power to control life. No one can determine that. I often say be fearless, say what you mean, say what you feel but I didn't do that with him. Mainly because I would experience him dissecting our reality and my words. With my words being challenged every step of the way it was often hard for me to express myself without the fear of it coming out wrong.

So I would run from my truth. I would keep my thoughts to myself until I felt I could express them correctly. My waiting resulted in what is allowing us to go on like we did. My fear in being different with him caused me to accept the incompleteness. I had constant quest to push people away. However, with my honesty and with my desire to be different with him I chose to pretend I was okay with him being with other women as long as I was with someone as well.

I am broken. I am damaged. I am fearful. I am stubborn. I am manipulative. I am controlling. I am afraid. I am definitely afraid because in life there is no right move. You just move and the outcome of it all is just that. The outcome.

So with him this is what I did. I stayed focused on staying true to my initial word. To stay unattached. However we both did the opposite of what that is. My admitting to my newly developed feelings was to cater to his desire of honesty. New things don't become a habit, you work on them and in the process of working on them you make mistakes.

And I hate that I am emotional. I hate that I care. Because I usually don't. I usually don't give a rat's ass. I don't even allow anyone to get close. But this one was different. He was different. I didn't seek it, I didn't pursue it, it just happened. He just came into my life one day and it all made sense. That was the difference. Because fate created it and I chose him; difference .

I sit here now and am courted, prodded, poked, queried, and pursued by man after man; guy after guy, boy after boy, and they all get compared to what was given to me. He was given to me. But why? That's the question! It hurts so much because I care. Ask me to turn my love off like a switch and I'll cry out I wish it was that easy.

I have two sides to me. With him I had two sides. The one where I loved him and together we were together, apart we were apart. The other side of me wanted to know him more, see him more, lead towards something better. But I didn't know what better was. But because I struggle with my words being dissected my speech became mute. I grew weak, I grew fearful, and I punked out. Truth is I knew I was punking out when I did it. It's my little way of ending it all I guess. I tend to push people away so that I won't get hurt.

I want him gone but then I don't. I don't because he is now a part of me. So many things add up to my saying, "I've waited 29 years for you to finally say hello." But now that he did say hello my goal is to NOT get hurt. To not get hurt is to say goodbye, right? Maybe I should just say goodbye.

Then you have him. Broken, guarded, and fearful just as I am. My recent actions have fueled elements of who he used to be. With me he was changing and so was I, but in the end we both have our ways of saying no to what was meant. My honesty was dissected. My main fear. My honesty was regretted. My second fear.

THE ![shit] I Didn't Say

And his commitment to stay in his ways changed us. The ultimate goal to be alone and not get hurt; right?

And I know that my goal will leave me broken and unhappy. But weirdly it's safe. I can go back to being the user, the promiscuous doll, the hardened shell, the manipulative player.

Love was evident and love is the one thing we BOTH run from. Maybe I could have pretended to not want more from him. You know fake it till I make it. Maybe eventually I wouldn't love him as much as I do.

Sadly though I will always love him and he knows it. And because I am me I don't give up so easily even when I am the one pushing the very thing I want away. I guess I should reallyyyyyyyyyyyy pick a side. Finally I did choose a side but the timing of it all may just be too late. But that's life. We can't control it. We should just have no regrets.

In spite of everything, I love you Janet.

Janet

Claire

"I miss you, every day that you are gone. I miss you it's fatal you know I am going to die without you." – J. Holiday

"I have to get out of this house Lewis. I am bored. I have been in here for two days straight," I studied Lewis who was standing over the stove cooking us some of his Mama's famous meatloaf as he called it.

"The doctor said for you to rest." He didn't turn to speak as he shot me down again.

I rolled my one good eye and blew out hot air. "I am medicated enough to not be in pain for at least three hours. Can I just feel the air on my skin perhaps?"

He turned and looked at me. "Claire you have cabin fever."

"Yes that's it cabin fever. Please." I begged like a school age girl and laughed. "I love being here with you but seriously take a sister out."

I heard the buzzing of my phone and noticed it was an unrecognizable number. Lewis turned to look at me and noticed my confusion and went to retrieve the phone to answer it instead of me. I had been fearful of answering my phone in case Evan was going to reach out. And in that case Lewis would answer for me.

"Hello!" he asked. I studied his face to catch any hints if it was Evan or not.

"Yes sir. Okay. Yes, we understand. Okay got it. We will be down at the station in half an hour. Okay, yes I understand. Okay see you soon." He sat my phone down and looked at me while releasing a deep breath. "They have Evan in custody. He's been officially caught babes." He leaned down and hugged me slowly as the words that he spoke leaped out at my heart and passed through my eyes. Tears.

"I'm safe?"

"You're safe." I fell into Lewis's arms and cried of a cry of relief. I had been on the edge ever since being released wondering if he was going to find me and now it was over.

Lewis bends down and kisses me slowly on my still bruised lip. "I love you!" I witnessed the tears in his eyes as he spoke his truths.

"I…I love you too," I replied truthfully. "I do so much," I cried.

"Let's go make an identification down at the station."

I nodded my head okay and picked up my phone and dialed Janet's number. It was now going to voicemail. I hung up confused and muttered, "I have been trying to get Janet on the phone for two days and now it's going to voicemail. I want to stop by her house on my way to the station."

Lewis nodded his head okay as I stood up slowly to make my way to the bathroom.

I stood in the mirror and studied my reflection. My face wasn't my face. I didn't witness my cinnamon brown skin, rose colored cheeks, my brown eyes that held a hint of gold, my hair pulled back into a common bun, my bottom lip still slightly swollen with scabs. Black and blue and scabbed was what I saw. He kissed me looking like this.

I ran my hands over my hair and took a deep breath. I was going to have to face Evan today. I was just grateful that it was at a police station. I took to my side of the closet that Lewis had given me and placed on some sweats, an oversized shirt, and my running shoes.

I heard Lewis walk up behind me. "How about tomorrow we go for a walk?"

I turned and smiled and took a deep breath. "I will go for an early morning walk if only you agree to return to work. I have to get back to writing myself."

He walked up to me, kissed my forehead and smiled. "Back to normalcy. Okay I agree."

I hugged and patted his butt. "Let's go soldier. Off to finish off justice. But first let's go see Janet."

We walked out of the house together, jumped into his car and hit the highway. I felt a sense of freedom and began to appreciate the simple things such as breathing fresh air God had blessed us with. Free air. I was free from the fear of Evan. I smiled brightly as I made my way to my girls house to tell her the good news.

Denim

"I was trippin'. I was dippin' with these women in these streets. Lost my girl. Lost all that. Wish I could take that back. You know that I love you but look at the damage I cause you. " – Chris Brown

It was the day I was to leave for Anguilla. Two days after I had allowed Janet to walk away. I didn't chase her because I didn't know what to say. I didn't want to beg either but I didn't want her to walk away. I didn't understand the level of pain that I had cause her until just now.

I missed her. I hadn't heard her voice. I hadn't seen her face. We hadn't touched each other. I needed that. I wanted all of those things. I felt like Jay Z when he said 'I was just fucking those women I was gone get right back'. Hell she knew that I loved her. Maybe if I just told her that we will be fine. But I would hate for her to give me an ultimatum.

It's been just a matter of months. I wasn't sure if I wanted to give up the other women, my freedom, and the power to do whatever I wanted just yet. It was too early to tell.

"When is it ever enough time to really know D?" I heard Dalvin's voice as I talked to him about my problems with Janet yesterday.

"What do you mean when is it enough time? The hell if I know."

"Dog don't come yelling at me. I'm your friend you know that. But I wouldn't be your friend if I just told you what you wanted to hear."

"Okay then say what it is that you want to say!" I sat across from him in one of our studios that I was burying myself in since I was pretty much trying to occupy my time.

"You can keep using that line but no one can truly place a time stamp on love dog. You have got to be willing to just go for it when it is given to you."

I rubbed my temples and studied the floor. "That's a big step man."

"Then why tell that woman you love her? How many women have you felt like this for?"

I grew quiet and pondered on his questions. "No one. Not since Nitrah."

"Exactly! And even for this woman you didn't want to give up your women, dog. Why is that? I ain't getting on you I am just asking."

I shrugged my shoulders refusing to look at him. "I don't know man."

"Yeah you know."

Jerking my head upward, I angrily said, "Since you know you tell me."

"Oh are you getting mad at your boy?" Dalvin asked, trying to get up under my skin.

"Dog just say what the hell you got to say. I am annoyed with this conversation."

"See that's your problem. You are stuck dog. You don't like to be told what to do, to be exposed to your bullshit and most of all you don't want to have a broken heart like you did after Nitrah. It's taken nearly fifteen years for you to find Janet and even then you do nothing. You allow yourself to stay stuck in your ways and somehow hurt her so what can happen? So you want have to get hurt."

I studied him and didn't speak.

"Yeah I know the game you're playing D. I was doing that after my marriage but I had to stop that. I was going to miss the chance to be happy. And dog you are fucking this up. I mean, why her friend? It's plenty of women out there."

I shrugged my shoulders and fell back into my seat. "Self-sabotage I guess."

"Exactly!"

THE ~~I~~ I Didn't Say

"Get up and make that work dog. Stop trying it your way for once. If it doesn't work, hey you tried and you dust yourself off and try again. D if you treated your love life like your music you would have never gotten here. When one door closed, he opened another and now look at you. Why can't you do that for this woman? You love her dog, I see it."

Yesterday's conversation was playing over and over in my head now as I made my way over to Janet's. I was going to present her with a ticket to go to Anguilla with me. I decided that I was going to at least take that step and then try something else new.

It was just time to be honest.

Janet

I sat in the window sill in my dining room and watched the wind blow through the trees in my backyard. I was listening to the sounds of the British band, Zero 7. I hadn't been in the mood to do much of anything lately. I couldn't even remember what day it was. I felt like I was floating. I felt like I was at peace with myself. Writing that letter to myself was therapeutic for me because everything I didn't say to Denim I placed on that piece of paper.

As I sat there and watched God's creation out my window I heard the sound of my screen door opening and then the front door knob turning. I heard Claire's voice call my name. I remembered I had given her a key to my house for emergencies and it had seemed now she was just letting herself in without warning.

I shot up from my seat. When I turned I saw her and Lewis walking through the door. "Hey what are you two doing here?"

Claire looked in my direction but she didn't lock eyes with me. Lewis stood behind her and looked around the living room and then said, "Look in her room!"

Confused, I laughed and said, "Ummm hello what are y'all doing here?" I began to walk towards them but they quickly brushed passed me and headed for my bedroom. What in the hell? Why are they acting like they cannot see me?

"Guys what the hell?" I yelled out behind them. I turned on my heels to walk into my room as well when I heard Claire scream out.

THE  I Didn't Say

"Oh my God, Janet! Janet can you hear me, wake up!" Her screams were so powerful I felt it in my womb. I felt my shoulders grow heavy as I rushed into the room to see what was wrong.

When I turned the corner I saw her and Lewis hovering over someone in my bed. "What the hell happened? What's going on?" I asked them. The fear was now evident in my voice as I grew fearful of what was happening. But again Lewis and Claire ignored me.

"She's cold Lewis, she's stiff and cold. Oh my God she's dead. She's dead!" Claire screams were deadly.

"I'm calling 911." Lewis hopped off the bed grabbing his phone out of his pocket and that's when I saw her. My heart dropped as I studied her face. My face. It was me.

I rushed to my bed and saw myself. I was there lying in my bed but how was I there when I was here?

"Claire?" I was crying asking her to answer me but it was clear she couldn't see or hear me.

Claire fell on top of me and cried out. She wept like a new born child her tears dropped on my silk pajamas and soaked them. I saw myself. I was much darker then I usually am. I looked at my eyes that were still open but they were as dark as the night. Nothing was there. You could clearly look into those eyes and tell a soul was missing. I noticed patterns of dried tears trace from my eyes down my cheeks. I had been crying.

I died! But how? Why?

I began to think back tuning out Claire's cries and then suddenly the sound of sirens as I tried to remember what had happened. My eyes locked in on my journal that lay on the bed beside me. I was writing. I was writing and then crying. And then I remembered the pain I felt in my chest as I thought about him. I remembered crying so hard that it hurt to breathe. I remember placing my journal down and lying back on my pillow to calm down. I remember now.

I remember my last breath.

He had broken my heart. He had caused so much pain that I couldn't bare it. The love I had for him overtook my heart and I drifted off. It made sense now why I hadn't wanted anything for what seemed like hours but were actually days. I wasn't of my mortal self. I was free. I was floating.

I felt my own tears drop down my cheeks as I witnessed paramedics rush in pulling Claire off of my body. She screamed and pulled on me but I was so stiff I didn't budge. I watched the paramedics look at me and call time of death.

I was lying dead in my bed but I felt that I had died the moment I couldn't tell Denim how I truly felt. Suddenly I turned when I heard his voice.

"What's going on?" Denim asked walking into my bedroom.

Claire noticed him walk in and Lewis shortly behind. Denim's eyes locked in on my body lying in the bed. I noticed him drop what was in his hand as he walked over towards me. His walk was zombie like, unreal and slow. He stood over six feet but it seems with each step he was shrinking.

"Babe!" he called out.

His eyes were swelling with tears. My body was trembling nearly in convulsions as I witnessed my love cry for his love. He fell onto the bed asking the paramedics to move to let him through. Bringing his hands to my face he studied me. "Babe wake up. Wake up babe. I got something to tell you." I had never heard Denim's voice like this.

It was husky and painful as he tried to talk through his tears. "Wake up babe. I love you. I love you so much," he cried.

I fell to my knees and cried. I had heard him say I love you before but never like this. It was as if he was telling me that his love meant more. That he wanted more, that I was it for him.

We cried. We all cried for what seemed like an eternity. Claire left to speak to the police as my sisters who had now arrived and were in my living room crying. I was walking around my house watching everyone. Watching everyone cry over my being gone.

THE ![stylized] I Didn't Say

The coroner had arrived and placed me in a bag and was now carrying me away. The visual forced Denim on his knees and he cried. He cried and held himself. "Why God, why her? Why her man? What the hell?"

I hurt for him. It hurt to watch him because I couldn't touch him. I couldn't talk to him. I noticed one of the paramedics examine my bed and then eye my journal. She read the top and said, "Denim?"

Denim looked over to her, "Yeah?"

"This has your name on it. Looks like it could be from Janet." She tried to sound compassionate as she handed it to him. "Doesn't look like foul play here by the way. She just simply died in her sleep. But we'll know more after an autopsy." She gave him her condolences and walked out of the room.

He slowly rose to his feet and repeated his zombielike walk from before and sat down on the window seal in my bedroom and studied the words on the paper.

I sat down on the floor in front of my door and watched him read. I felt a piece pf paper underneath me and scooted over to look at it.

My eyes zoomed in on words that said First Class. It was a ticket to Anguilla with my name on it. My mouth dropped and I screamed out in disbelief. He was going to take me with him.

I closed my eyes and cried when I felt myself began to move. I opened my eyes and noticed everything around was white, it was bright; it wasn't my home any more. I wasn't there anymore. I couldn't see them now. I had floated off into what had to be the heavens. It was all done. My life was done.

For him and me it was too late. I didn't plan on dying of a broken heart but then again I didn't plan on loving someone so much either.

Denim

Denim,

If I could do it all over again I would just admit that I loved you. I would just tell you that I only wanted you. I wish I could go back to the very beginning when we first met and look into your eyes and ask, "Do you feel that connection? Do you sense that something is going on between us that isn't normal?"

Our love wasn't normal. We knew each other before we ever knew each other but we were too stuck to admit it. We were too stuck to just allow love to be love without creating boundaries and rules. I love you. I breathe you. I need you. I wanted nothing more but you. I don't know why that was so hard to say.

I guess my fear was that in spite of telling you these things you wouldn't care anyway. I know you loved me but I think you loved what you wanted more .Which was freedom. I wasn't enough for you. I don't know if I would had ever been enough but we never tried it to see.

I could handle you being with other women because I knew I had your heart but why should I have to hide that I changed my mind? I changed my mind Denim! I didn't want any other man but you. I only wanted you now. That isn't fearful to hear right? Someone telling you that they love you and that they only want you should be one of the most beautiful messages you could ever be told.

But you weren't willing to try. You told me about your women, your trips, and your exploits as if I was your homeboy. If you loved me so much like you said you did, why wasn't I enough? Why weren't you willing to see about you and I?

THE I Didn't Say

You took my heartbeat from me. You became a part of me. I loved you. I just wish I were enough. I am sorry I was never bold enough to tell you how I feel. I just was afraid of pushing you away. But the next time I have a chance at love I will never fear fighting for it. The saddest story anyone can have is to have loved someone and to have never told them.

Well let me tell you that I love you. I wanted to be the one to make you happy. Why not choose me? Choose us? Why not choose difference? You took my heartbeat from me, was it because I loved you poorly?

I'll always love you!

Love Janet

I gripped her journal so tightly that I couldn't even feel it in my hands any longer. I was in pain. I was confused. The last time couldn't be the last time. This can't be my story.

Her journal fell to my feet as I witness the coroner place her body in their truck. My tears clouded my vision as I whispered the words, "I will always love you too."

Also in Stores

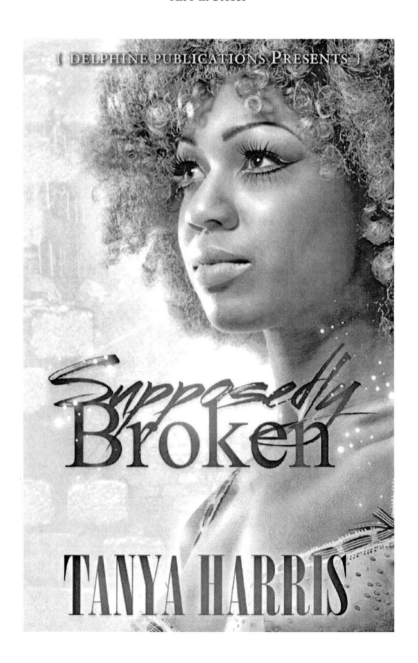

[DELPHINE PUBLICATIONS PRESENTS]

Supposedly
Broken

TANYA HARRIS

{ DELPHINE PUBLICATIONS PRESENTS }

"She is willing to pay the ultimate price,
but she never thought she would lose everything...
even her own life."

Love
on Death Row

MELISSA LOVE

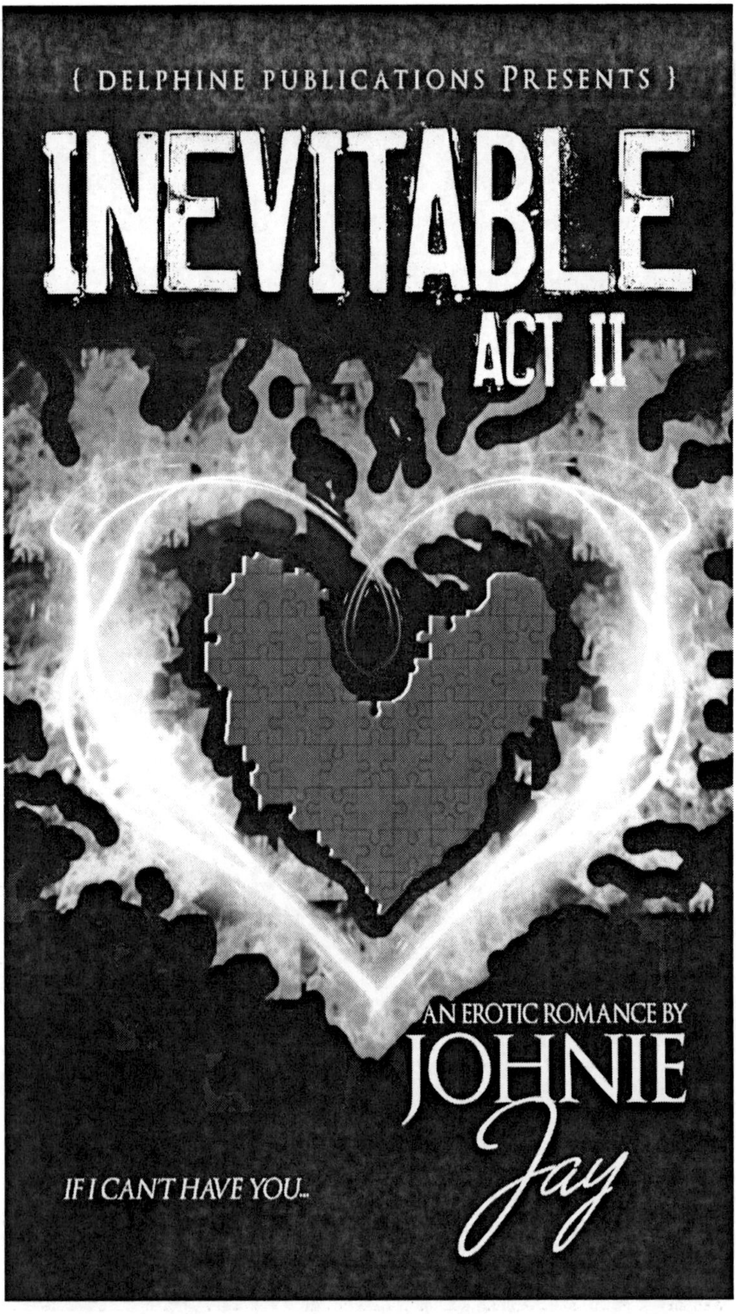
{ DELPHINE PUBLICATIONS PRESENTS }
INEVITABLE
ACT II
AN EROTIC ROMANCE BY
JOHNIE
Jay
IF I CAN'T HAVE YOU...

Coming soon from

If I Ain't THE ONE You LOVE

A KISSES DON'T LIE NOVEL

"Sure men come and go but friends do too"

TAMIKA NEWHOUSE

AUTHOR OF *KISSES DON'T LIE*

CPSIA information can be obtained at www.ICGtesting.com
Printed in the USA
LVOW05s2141050814

397736LV00013B/152/P

9 780996 084499